Shakespeare's Landlord

Also by Charlaine Harris

Aurora Teagarden Mysteries
Sleep Like a Baby
All the Little Liars
Poppy Done to Death
Last Scene Alive
A Fool and His Honey
Dead Over Heels
The Julius House
Three Bedrooms, One Corpse
A Bone to Pick
Real Murders

Lily Bard Mysteries
Shakespeare's Counselor
Shakespeare's Trollop
Shakespeare's Christmas
Shakespeare's Champion

**Sookie Stackhouse/
True Blood Novels**
After Dead
Dead Ever After
Deadlocked
Dead Reckoning
Dead in the Family

Dead and Gone
From Dead to Worse
All Together Dead
Definitely Dead
Dead as a Doornail
Dead to the World
Club Dead
Living Dead in Dallas
Dead Until Dark

Harper Connelly Mysteries
Grave Secret
An Ice Cold Grave
Grave Surprise
Grave Sight

**Cemetery Girl Trilogy
(with Christopher Golden)**
Inheritance
The Pretenders

Midnight, Texas Novels
Night Shift
Day Shift
Midnight Crossroad

Shakespeare's Landlord

Charlaine Harris

Minotaur Books
New York

SHAKESPEARE'S LANDLORD. Copyright © 1996 by Charlaine Harris. All rights reserved. Printed in the United States of America. For information, address St. Martin's Press, 175 Fifth Avenue, New York, N.Y. 10010.

www.minotaurbooks.com

The Library of Congress has cataloged the hardcover edition as follows:

Harris, Charlaine
   Shakespeare's landlord / by Charlaine Harris.—1st ed.
     p. cm.
   "A Thomas Dunne Book."
   ISBN 0-312-14415-9
   1. Woman detectives—Arkansas—Fiction. I. Title.
   PS3558.A6427 S
   813'.54—dc30   96–6224
                                          CIP

ISBN 978-1-250-10728-2 (trade paperback)

Our books may be purchased in bulk for promotional, educational, or business use. Please contact your local bookseller or the Macmillan Corporate and Premium Sales Department at 1-800-221-7945, extension 5442, or by email at MacmillanSpecialMarkets@macmillan.com.

First Minotaur Books Paperback Edition: April 2018

10 9 8 7 6 5 4 3 2 1

For all my fellow inmates
in Doctor Than's House of Pain:
especially Martha, John, and Wayne

One

I gathered myself, my bare feet gripping the wooden floor, my thigh muscles braced for the attack. I stepped forward on the ball of my left foot, pivoting as I moved, and my right leg swung up, bent at the knee. My foot lashed out, returned instantly. The black Everlast punching bag rocked on its chain.

My right foot touched down, and I pivoted lightly on the ball of that foot, my body oriented this time facing the bag. My left leg came forward to deliver a longer, harder, thrusting mae geri. I continued the kicking, the pivoting, alternating the side kicks with the front kicks, practicing my weaker back kicks, my breathing growing deeper but never losing its rhythm—exploding out with the kick, coming in deep with the retraction.

The bag danced on the end of its chain, swinging back and forth, requiring more and more concentration on my part to plant the next kick accurately. I was tiring.

Finally, I lashed out with my stronger right leg, using all my power, dodged the backswing, and struck seiken, my hand in a smooth line with my arm, my knuckles driving into the bag.

I had finished my exercise. Automatically, I bowed, as I would have if I'd had a live sparring partner, and shook my head in disgust at my own foolishness. I reached for the towel hanging on its appointed hook by the doorknob. As I patted my face, I wondered whether my workout had been enough; if I took a shower now and got in bed, would I sleep? It was worth a try.

I washed my hair, soaped and rinsed, and was out within five minutes. After I dried myself, I put mousse on my hair and stood before the mirror to fluff it out with my fingers and a pick; I had tucked the towel around me so I couldn't see my chest in the mirror.

My hair is short and light blond now. One of my few extravagances is getting it colored, permed, and cut at Terra Ann's, the fanciest hairdressing salon in Shakespeare. Some of my employers get their hair done there; they never know quite what to say when they see me.

Most bodybuilders consider a deep tan part of their regimen, but I'm pale. The scarring doesn't stand out so much that way. But I do get rid of excess hair; I pluck every stray eyebrow, and my legs and armpits are shaved smooth as a baby's bottom.

Once upon a time, years ago, I thought I was pretty. My sister, Varena, and I had the usual rivalry going, and I remember deciding my eyes were bigger and a lighter blue than hers, my nose was straighter and thinner, and my lips were fuller. Her chin was better—neat and determined. Mine is round. I haven't seen Varena in three years now. Probably she is the pretty one. Though my face hasn't changed, my mind has. The workings of the mind look out through the face and alter it.

Sometimes, some mornings—the ones after the really bad nights—I look in the mirror and do not recognize the woman I see there.

This was going to be one of those really bad nights (though I had no idea how bad it was going to get). But I could tell there was no point in going to bed. My feet itched to be moving.

I dressed again, throwing my sweaty workout clothes into the hamper and pulling on blue jeans and a T-shirt, tucking in the T-shirt and pulling a belt through the belt loops. My hair was only a little damp; the blow-dryer finished the job. I pulled on a dark windbreaker.

Front door, back door, kitchen door? Some nights it takes me a while to decide.

The back. Though I keep my doors greased so they swing back and forth almost noiselessly, the back door is the quietest.

The back door is directly opposite the front door, making my house a shotgun house; from my back door, I can look down the hall and through the living room, which occupies the width of the front of the house, to check to make sure the dead bolt is shot.

It was, of course; I am not one to neglect security. I locked the back door as I left, using another key to turn the dead bolt from the outside. I pushed the key down to the very bottom of my front pocket, where it couldn't possibly fall out. I stood on the tiny back porch for a minute, inhaling the faint scent of the new leaves on the climbing rose vines. The vines were halfway up the trellis I'd built to make the little porch prettier.

Of course, it also obstructed my view of anyone approaching, but when the first roses open in about a month, I won't regret it. I have loved roses since I was a child; we lived on a large lot in a small town, and roses filled the backyard.

That yard of my childhood was easily five times as big as this backyard, which extends less than twenty feet, ending abruptly in a steep slope up to the railroad tracks. The slope is covered with weeds, but from time to time a work crew wanders through to keep the weeds under control. To my left as I faced the tracks was the high wooden privacy fence that surrounded the Shakespeare Garden Apartments. It's slightly uphill from my house. To my right, and downhill, was the equally tiny backyard of the only other house on the street. It's nearly an exact copy of my house, and it's owned by an accountant named Carlton Cockroft.

Carlton's lights were off, not too surprising at this hour of the night. The only light I could see in the apartment building was in Deedra Dean's place. As I glanced up, her window fell dark.

One o'clock in the morning.

I silently stepped off my little back porch, my walking shoes making almost no noise in the grass, and began to move invisibly through the streets of Shakespeare. The night was still and dark—no wind, the moon only a crescent in cold space. I could not even see myself. I liked that.

An hour and a half later, I felt tired enough to sleep.

I was on my way home, and I was not trying to conceal myself anymore; in fact, I was being sloppy. I was using the sidewalk that borders the arboretum (a fancy name for an overgrown park with some labels on trees and bushes). Estes Arboretum takes up a block of definitely unprime Shakespeare real estate. Each of the four streets edging the park has a different name, and my street, Track, on the park's east side, is only a block long. So there's little traffic, and every morning I get to look out my front window and see trees across the street instead of someone else's carport.

I rounded the corner from the south side of the arboretum, Latham Street, to Track; I was opposite the little piece of scrubland that no one claimed, just south of Carlton Cockroft's house. I was not careless enough to linger under the weak streetlight at the corner. There is one at each corner of the arboretum, as Shakespeare's budget can't run to putting streetlights in the middle of the block, especially in this obscure part of town.

I hadn't seen a soul all night, but suddenly I was aware I was not alone. Someone was stirring in the darkness on the other side of the street.

Instinctively, I concealed myself, sliding behind a live oak on the edge of the park. Its branches overhung the sidewalk; perhaps their shadow had hidden me from the presence across the street. My heart was pounding unpleasantly fast. Some tough woman you are, I jeered at myself. What would Marshall think if he saw you now? But when I'd had a second to calm down, I decided that Marshall might think I was showing some sense.

I peered around the oak's trunk cautiously. In the middle of the block, where the person was, the darkness was almost total; I couldn't even tell if I was watching a man or a woman. I had a flash of an unpleasant recollection: my great-grandmother, in the act of saying, "Blacker than a nigger in a coal mine with his mouth shut," and embarrassing everyone in the whole family quite unconsciously. Or maybe not; maybe that little nod of satisfaction had not been over a well-turned phrase but over the pained looks she'd intercepted passing between my parents.

My great-grandmother would have stomped out to the middle of the street and inquired what the person's business was, quite assured of her own safety in doing so, too.

But I know better.

The person was pushing something, something on wheels.

Peering intently into the darkness, I tried to remember if I'd ever seen anyone out on my street before when I was up and wandering. I'd seen a few cars go by, residents or visitors of people in the apartment building, but I couldn't recall ever meeting up with anyone on foot in the past four years—at least in this part of town.

On the bad nights, when I ghost all the way downtown, it is sometimes a different story.

But here and now, I had something to worry about. There was something furtive about this odd incident; this person, this other inhabitor of the night, was pushing what I could now tell was a cart, one with two wheels. It had a handle in the middle of the longer side, and legs on it, so that when you let go of the handle and set it upright, it would be steady and straight. And it was just the right size for two thirty-gallon garbage cans.

My hands curled into fists. Even in the dark, I could identify the familiar shape of the cart. It was my own. I'd bought it at a yard sale from some people who were moving; the man of the house had made it himself.

It was loaded down with something wrapped in dark plastic, like the sheets you buy to put in flower beds to keep weeds down; I could see the faint shine off the smooth plastic surface.

I felt a rage I hadn't experienced in a long time. Something illicit was happening, and the cart thief was trying to involve me in it. The peace that I'd worked so hard to achieve was going to be ripped away, through no fault of my own. I could not confront this thief directly; that wouldn't make sense—the thief might be armed, and was obviously in the middle of doing something he or she wanted to conceal.

So I clenched my teeth, and watched and waited.

Across the rough surface of neglected Track Street, the thief trundled my garbage-can cart with its heavy burden; I could tell it was heavy because of the strain in the cart thief's posture.

This was absolutely eerie; I found myself shivering. I pulled the sides of my dark windbreaker together and, with a tiny sound, zipped it shut. With deliberate movements, I pulled a thin dark scarf from my pocket and tied it over my light hair. All the while, I was tracking the cart thief's laborious progress. The thief was heading for the park; I felt my lips twitch up in a smile as I observed the thief trying to get the cart from the pavement up onto the sidewalk. Wheelchair accessibility had not been a priority when those sidewalks were paved many years ago.

Finally, the cart bumped up onto the sidewalk and across it. The thief's feet had to hurry to catch up. Into the darkness of the arboretum, following one of the narrow paved paths, the thief rolled the loaded cart. I began to count seconds. In three minutes, the thief returned, still pushing my cart.

Now it was empty.

My anger was taking second place to curiosity, though that would only be temporary.

I watched the thief roll the cart up my driveway, barely making it through the narrow walk space between my car and the carport wall. The thief reappeared from the back of my house, walking quickly, and had to go down my driveway to the curb and then walk around the end of the fence to walk up the apartment building's south driveway. The thief circled around back; he or she would enter the building through the quieter back door; the front door squeaked. I always remember things like that.

I am in and out of that apartment building quite a lot.

Sure enough, the thief didn't reappear at the other side of the apartment building. It was someone living there, or the overnight guest of someone living there. With one single woman and four single men living there, overnight guests are not infrequent.

For a few more seconds, I hugged close to the trunk of the tree, waiting to see if a light would come on. From where I was, I could see the side windows on the south side of the apartment building and the front windows, too; no lights came on in any of them. Someone was being extra careful.

Well, I, too, would be careful. I waited five minutes, according to my digital watch, before I made a move. Then I went deeper into the arboretum, following no trail, moving as quietly as possible in the darkness. I'd estimated where I'd intersect the path; I was as familiar with the layout of the arboretum as I was with the floor plan of my house. I'd spent hours wandering Shakespeare by night.

It was so black in the thick of the trees that I wondered if I would even be able to find what the thief had dumped. If my jeans hadn't brushed the plastic, which emitted that typical dry rustle, I might have groped around the path for another hour.

But the second I heard that rustle, I dropped to my hands and knees. Patting around in the darkness, I discovered the wrapping was not plastic sheeting but two large garbage bags, one pulled from the top and another from the bottom to overlap in the middle covering—something soft and big. I poked the bag; there was something hard under the softness. Something bumpy. Something an awful lot like ribs.

I bit my lower lip to keep from making noise.

I struggled silently with an almost-overwhelming urge to jump up and run. After several deep breaths, I won. I steeled myself to do what I had to do, but I couldn't face doing it in the dark.

I reached into my windbreaker pocket and pulled out a narrow, lightweight, powerful little flashlight that had caught my fancy at Wal-Mart. I shifted in my squatting position so that my body was between the apartment building and what was on the ground. I switched on the flashlight.

I was angry at myself when I saw my hand was shaking as I separated the bags. I fumbled them apart some four inches and stopped. I was looking at a torn, rather faded shirt, a man's plaid shirt in green and orange. The chest pocket had caught on something; it was partially ripped from its stitching and a fragment was missing.

I recognized the shirt, though it hadn't been torn when I'd seen it last.

I worked the bag up a little at the side and found a hand; I put my fingers on the wrist, where a pulse should be.

In the chilly Shakespeare night, I squatted in the middle of the trees, holding hands with a dead man.

And now I'd left my fingerprints all over the plastic bags.

About forty minutes later, I was sitting in my bedroom. I was finally tired to the bone.

I'd taken the bags off the corpse.

I'd confirmed the corpse's identity, and its corpsedom. No breath, no heartbeat.

I'd worked my way out of the arboretum, knowing I was leaving traces but helpless to avoid it. My incoming traces were unerasable; I'd figured I might as well make a trail out, too. I'd emerged from the bushes on Latham and crossed the street there, well out of sight of the apartments. I'd gone from cover to cover until I circled Carlton Cockroft's house, silently crossing his yard to arrive in my own.

I'd found that the cart thief had replaced my cart and reinserted the garbage cans, but not as I'd had them. The blue garbage can was always on the right and the brown on the left, and the thief had reversed them. I'd unlocked my back door and entered without turning on a light, then opened the correct kitchen drawer, extracted two twisties, and lifted out and sealed the garbage bags already lining the cans. I'd relined the cans with the garbage bags that had been used to cover the body, then put the bagged garbage in them, sealing the second set of bags over the first set. I'd figured I couldn't examine the cart in the middle of the night, and wheeling it inside would have created too much noise. It would have to wait until morning.

I'd done all I could do to erase my own involuntary complicity.

I should have been ready for bed, but I found myself biting my lower lip. My bedrock middle-class upbringing was raising its strong and stern head, as it did at unexpected and inconvenient times. The mortal remains of someone I knew were lying out there in dark solitude. That was wrong.

I couldn't call the police department; possibly incoming calls were taped or traced in some way, even in little Shakespeare. Maybe I could just forget about it? Someone would find him in the morning. But it might be the little kids who lived on Latham. . . . And then it came to me—whom I could call. I hesitated, my fingers twisting and untwisting. The back of my neck told me this was not a smart move. Get it over with, I told myself.

I pulled out my little flashlight again and was able to read my tiny Shakespeare phone book by its dimming glow. I punched in the right numbers, listened to three rings; then a groggy male voice said, "Claude Friedrich here."

"Listen," I said, surprised at how harsh and ragged my voice came out. I waited a beat.

"Okay." He was alert now.

"There's a dead man in the park across the street from you," I said, and hung up the phone. I crept across the hall to the room with the punching bag, my workout room. Through its window, I could see the light come on in Claude Friedrich's apartment, which was on the second floor, by Deedra Dean's.

Now I'd done all I could.

With a pleasant feeling of having discharged a responsibility, I climbed out of my clothes and into a nightgown. I heard a car in the street outside, and I padded into my dark living room to look out the window. Friedrich had taken my phone call seriously; he was out there in hastily thrown-on clothes, talking to one of the night patrolmen, Tom David Meikle-john. As I watched, they started down the same path into the park that the cart thief had taken, each carrying a powerful "skull-buster" flashlight.

Incident closed, I thought, going back to my bedroom and crawling into my double bed. I pulled the fresh sheets up, settled my head on my pillow, and instantly, finally, fell asleep.

Two

The next day was a Tuesday. On Tuesday mornings, I take care of Mrs. Hofstettler. Marie Hofstettler's son Chuck lives in Memphis. He worries about his mother, but he doesn't worry enough to make the drive over to Shakespeare to see her. So he pays me handsomely to spend time with his mother twice a week.

I always do a little cleaning, channel Mrs. Hofstettler's clothes through the washer and dryer, and occasionally take her to a friend's house or K Mart or Kroger's, if Mrs. Hofstettler is having what she calls a "limber" day.

I walked over from my house to the apartment building, letting myself in the squeaking front door and rapping lightly on the first door to my left to let Mrs. Hofstettler know I was coming in. I had a key. Mrs. Hofstettler was already up, a good sign; on her bad, stiff days, she is still in bed when I get there.

"I didn't sleep at all last night!" she said by way of greeting. Marie Hofstettler, now eighty-five, is as wrinkled as a dried apricot. Her hair is white and silky and thin, and she wears it pulled back in an untidy bun. (I know what pain it costs the old lady to raise her arms to form the bun. In a stu-pid moment, I had suggested Mrs. Hofstettler have her hair cut short, and I had been treated to a huffy hour-long silence.) This morning, Mrs. Hofstettler's teeth were already in and she had managed to pull on a red-and-blue-striped housedress, so the excitement had done her good.

"I saw there was crime-scene tape across the path going into the park," I commented in as neutral a voice as I could man-age. No true Shakespearean would call Estes Arboretum any-thing but "the park." I'm finally getting the hang of being a true Shakespearean after four years.

"Didn't you hear all the commotion, girl?"

"I didn't hear a thing," I answered truthfully. "I slept real heavy last night." I went down the hall to Mrs. Hofstettler's bedroom to fetch the wash from the hamper.

"Then you are an amazing sleeper," Mrs. Hofstettler called after me. "Honey, there were police cars up and down the street, and people coming and going, and an ambulance, too."

"And I don't know anything about it to tell you," I said, trying to sound regretful. I'm not normally chatty with cli-ents, but I admire Marie Hofstettler; she doesn't whine and she isn't clingy.

"Let's turn on the radio," Mrs. Hofstettler said eagerly. "Maybe we can find out what happened. If that don't work, I'm calling Deedra at the courthouse. She always knows what's going on."

I started the washing machine. All eight apartments, of course, have the same layout, with the east apartments mir-roring the west. There are four units upstairs and four down-stairs. The building's front door and back door are locked at eleven, and residents aren't supposed to give anyone a key.

Marie's apartment is a ground-floor front apartment on the north side. She's had it since the building was erected ten years ago; Marie and Pardon Albee are the only original tenants. In Marie's apartment, as in all of them, the common hallway door opens directly into a living room, with an area to the rear used for dining. Across from this dining area is the kitchen, of course, which is well lined with cabinets and counters for an apartment kitchen. The hall starts where the kitchen and dining area end, and to your right (in Marie's apartment) is the closet containing the washer and dryer and shelves used for linens and cleaners and odds and ends. Almost opposite this closet is the door to the master bedroom, which is a nice size and has a very large closet. On the same wall as the wash closet is the door to the much smaller guest bedroom, and at the end of the hall is the bathroom, with a large frosted-glass window, which is supposed to be the second line of escape in case of fire.

I've always appreciated the fact that the front doors are not centered, so that when a tenant answers his or her front door, the caller can't see down the hall directly into the bathroom.

The builder and resident landlord, Pardon Albee, had had the gall to call these the Shakespeare Garden Apartments because the front ones overlook the arboretum. The back ones at the ground floor overlook only the paved area that lies between the apartment and the garage, divided into eight stalls not quite wide enough for two cars each. The second floor apartments at the back have a scenic view of the train tracks, and beyond them the back lot of a hardware and lumber-supply store.

After I'd turned on the radio for Mrs. Hofstettler, I began dusting the larger bedroom. Mrs. Hofstettler turned up the radio loud so I could listen along, after a conscientious discussion about whom it might bother; no one, the old woman decided, since T. L. and Alvah York next door should be out for their morning walk, and Norvel Whitbread, whose apartment was above, was already at work, or drunk, or both.

The area station, which covered most of Hartsfield and Creek counties, plays so-called classic rock. It is a preprogrammed station. The song that came on first was one I'd liked long ago, before the time when my life's agenda had gotten so . . . simplified. I smiled as I lifted the old china figurines on the dressing table and dusted them very carefully. The song ended, I glanced at my watch, and right on cue the local announcer began to speak, her southern Arkansas accent so broad that even after four years in Shakespeare, I had to listen quite carefully.

"In local news" ("In lawcol nyus"), twanged the conscientiously serious voice, "in Hartsfield County, Shakespeare real estate developer Pardon Albee was found dead in Estes Arboretum at approximately two-thirty A.M. by Police Chief Claude Friedrich, who was acting on an anonymous phone tip. The cause of death is not known at this time, but police suspect foul play. Albee was a lifelong resident of Shakespeare and a member of the Shakespeare Combined Church. In other news, a Creek County judge sentenced Harley Don Murrell to twenty years for the abduction and rape of a local—"

"Oh no!" Mrs. Hofstettler exclaimed in real distress.

I carefully put down the shepherdess I'd been dusting and hurried into the living room. "Lily, this is horrible! Oh, Lily, do you suppose he was killed and robbed right here? And who will we pay rent to now that Pardon Albee's dead? Who'll own the building?"

I automatically handed Mrs. Hofstettler a Kleenex, thinking it was very like her to come right to the point. Who indeed owned the building now? When I'd recognized Pardon Albee's ugly green-and-orange plaid shirt last night, that hadn't been what I'd thought of.

The answer would not affect me directly, for I'd bought my house from Pardon, as had my neighbor. And Pardon had sold the lots at the north end of Track and around the corner on Jamaica Street to the Shakespeare Combined Church, a coalition of splinter churches that had thrived most unexpectedly. As far as I knew, the only property that Pardon still owned outright was Shakespeare Garden Apartments, and he'd enjoyed owning it to the hilt. In fact, he'd seen himself as the pivotal character in some kind of television drama—the kindly landlord who helps all his tenants solve their problems and knows all their most intimate secrets.

He'd worked hard on making the last part come true, anyway.

"I've got to call—Lily, I'm so glad you're here today!"

Mrs. Hofstettler was more upset than I'd ever seen her, and I'd heard her fume for two weeks over the altar boy at St. Stephen's Episcopal Church lighting the wrong candle during Advent.

"Who did you want to call?" I asked, putting down the dust cloth.

"The police. Pardon was here yesterday. It was the first of the month, you know. I get a check from Chuck toward the end of the month, and I deposit it, and every first, here comes Mr. Albee, regular as clockwork. I always have my check made out and sitting on the table for him, and he always . . . Oh, I think I should tell the police he was here!"

"I'll call, then." I hoped Mrs. Hofstettler could ease her agitation with a phone call. To my surprise and dismay, the dispatcher at the Shakespeare Police Department said someone would be right by to listen to Mrs. Hofstettler's story.

"You'd better make some coffee, Lily, please," the old lady said. "Maybe the policeman will want some. Oh, what could have happened to Pardon? I can't believe it. Just yesterday, he was standing right *there*. And now he's dead, and him a good twenty-five years younger than me! And Lily, could you pick up that tissue there, and straighten that pillow on the sofa? Oh, durn these stiff old legs! You just don't know, Lily, how frustrating being old can be."

There was no safe response to that, so I straightened the room very quickly. The coffee was perking, everything in the apartment was dusted, and I'd given the bathroom a quick once-over by the time the doorbell rang. I was pulling the clothes from the dryer, but I'd become infected by Marie's house-pride, so I hastily carried the clean wash back to deposit in the guest bedroom and shut the louver doors that concealed the washer and dryer on my way back to answer the bell.

I had expected some underling. With a pang of dismay, I recognized the chief of police, the man I'd called in the middle of the night, Claude Friedrich.

I stood aside and waved him in, cursing my conscience-stricken call, afraid anything I said would cause him to recognize my voice.

It was the first time I'd seen Claude Friedrich close up, though of course I had glimpsed him driving in and out of the apartment house driveway, and occasionally passed him in the hall when I was in the building on a cleaning job.

Claude Friedrich was in his late forties, a very tall man with a deep tan, light brown hair and mustache streaked with gray, and light gray eyes that shown in the weathered face. He had few wrinkles, but the ones he had were so deep, they might have been put in with a chisel. He had a broad face and a square jaw, broad shoulders and hands, a flat stomach. His gun looked very natural on his hip. The dark blue uniform made my mouth feel dry, made something inside me twitch with anxiety, and I reacted with anger.

Macho man, I thought. As if he could hear me, Friedrich suddenly turned to catch me with my brows raised, one side of my mouth pulled up sardonically. We locked stares for a tense moment.

"Mrs. Hofstettler," he said politely, transferring his gaze to my employer, who was twisting a handkerchief in her hands.

"Thank you for coming—maybe you didn't even need to," Mrs. Hofstettler said in one breath. "I would hate to bother you. Please have a seat." She gestured toward the flowered sofa at right angles to the television and to her own favorite recliner.

"Thank you, ma'am, and coming here is no trouble at all," Friedrich said comfortingly. He knew how to be soothing, no doubt about it. He sat down gratefully, as if he'd been standing for a long time. I moved into the kitchen, which has a hatch cut in the wall behind the counter, and opened it to stick out the coffeepot behind our guest's back. Mrs. Hofstettler, thus reminded, went into her hostess mode, helping her regain her calm.

"I'm not being polite," Mrs. Hofstettler accused herself, turning her mild, faded blue eyes on her guest. "Please, have some coffee. Do you take cream and sugar?"

"Thanks," Friedrich said. "I'd love some coffee. Black, please."

"Lily, would you mind bringing Chief Friedrich some black coffee? I don't believe I want any. But you get yourself a cup and come join us. I believe, young man, that I knew your father. . . ." And Mrs. Hofstettler was off on the inevitable establishing of connections that made southern introductions so cosy and drawn-out.

Knowing it would please Mrs. Hofstettler, I fixed a tray with napkins, a plate of cookies (a secret indulgence of Marie's—she likes Keebler Elves, chocolate with chocolate filling), and two generous cups of coffee. While I was assembling the tray, I was listening to Friedrich telling Marie about his years as a police officer in Little Rock; his decision to return to Shakespeare when, in quick succession, his father died, he himself divorced his wife, and the position of chief of police became vacant; and his pleasure at rediscovering the slower pace of life in little Shakespeare.

This guy was good.

As I aligned the napkins in overlapping triangles on the brightly painted tole tray, I admitted to myself that I was worried. After all, how long could I go without speaking before it looked just plain peculiar? On the other hand, he'd been asleep when I'd made the call. And I'd said so little, maybe he wouldn't recognize my voice?

I lifted the tray easily and carried it out to the living room. I handed Friedrich his cup. Now that I was close to him again, I was even more aware of how big he was.

"I'm sorry, I don't believe I've actually met you. . . ." Friedrich said delicately as I perched on the hard armchair opposite him.

"Oh, you'll have to excuse me!" Mrs. Hofstettler said ruefully, shaking her head. "This awful news has just taken away all my manners. Chief Friedrich, this is *Miss* Lily Bard. She lives in the house next to our apartment building, and Lily has become the mainstay of Shakespeare since she moved here."

Trust Mrs. Hofstettler not to ignore a matchmaking opportunity; I should have anticipated this.

"I've seen you around, of course," the big man said, with the courtly implication that no man could ignore me.

"I clean Deedra Dean's apartment," I said briefly.

"Did you work in this building yesterday?"

"Yes."

He waited for me to continue. I didn't.

"Then we need to talk later, when you're not working," he said gently, as if he was talking to a shaky centenarian, or a mental deficient.

I nodded curtly. "I have a break between four and five-thirty."

"I'll come to your house then," he said, and without giving me any time to agree or disagree, he focused his light gray eyes on his hostess.

"Now, Miss Marie, you tell me about seeing Mr. Albee yesterday."

"Well," Mrs. Hofstettler said slowly, gathering herself together with a kind of morbid pleasure, "Pardon always comes about nine in the morning on the first day of the month . . . to collect the rent. I know he likes the other tenants to stop by his apartment, but he comes to me because I have limber days and I have stiff days, and I never know till I open my eyes in the morning which it's going to be." She shook her head at the vagaries of illness and old age, and Friedrich responded with a sympathetic rumble.

"So he rang the doorbell, and I let him in," Mrs. Hofstettler said, concentrating hard on her narrative. "He was wearing an orange-and-green plaid shirt and dark green polyester pants . . . kind of bad colors for anyone, but for a fair man, really not . . . well, that's neither here nor there. But especially if you're kind of heavyset . . . well . . . So he commented on the weather, and I answered—you know, the usual kind of thing people say to old ladies they don't know very well!"

Claude Friedrich smiled at this particular sharp old lady, took a sip of his coffee, then raised his cup to me in silent appreciation.

"Did he say anything about his plans for the day?" the police chief rumbled. His voice was like the sound of far-off thunder; it made you feel quite safe right where you were.

I was *really* going to have to be careful. I stared down into my coffee cup. I was so angry that I'd embroiled myself in the death of Pardon Albee, I pictured myself hurling the coffee cup against Mrs. Hofstettler's dead-white wall. Of course, I wouldn't; Marie was not to blame for my predicament. I sighed silently, then looked up to meet Claude Friedrich's intent gaze. Damn.

"He just said he had to go back to his place to wait for everyone to come by with the rent. Since you've been living here, Mr. Friedrich, you know how Pardon was about getting the rent right on the dot. He did say something about interesting things on the news. . . ."

"Local news? National news?" Friedrich queried gently. He wasn't breaking into Mrs. Hofstettler's stream of thought, I observed. He was more directing it with a gentle insinuation every now and then. It was skillful. And I noticed that somehow he'd managed to make two cookies vanish, without my ever seeing him chew.

"He didn't say." Marie Hofstettler shook her head regretfully. "He was kind of cheerful about it, though. You know, Pardon was—I don't know how to say it, now that he's gone—he liked to know things," she finished delicately, with a tiny contraction of her brows and a little bob of her head.

He had called it "taking a neighborly interest."

That wasn't what I had called it.

"Now, yesterday, did you see any of your neighbors here?" Friedrich asked Mrs. Hofstettler.

She thought, her lips pursed.

"I thought once I heard Alvah and T. L. next door, but they weren't due to come in until late last night, so I must have been mistaken. And I heard people knocking on Mr. Albee's door—to pay their rent, you know—several times during the morning and afternoon. But I'm almost always watching the TV or playing the radio, and I don't hear quite as well as I used to."

"When you thought you heard the Yorks, do you mean you heard their voices, enough to identify them, or do you mean that you just heard someone next door?"

Again, Mrs. Hofstettler thought carefully. "I believe I just heard movement next door."

"It might have been me," I said. "I bought some groceries for them and put them in the kitchen and was supposed to water the plant."

"Well, I heard this sound about three in the afternoon. I'd just gotten up from my nap."

"That was probably me."

Friedrich made a note in a little hot-pink spiral-bound notebook that suddenly appeared in his hands.

I glanced at my watch. I had to leave in thirty minutes to get to my next cleaning job, and I had yet to put away Marie's clean laundry.

"Excuse me," I murmured, and took the tray back to the kitchen, feeling Friedrich's bright gaze on my back. I quickly washed and dried the dishes, then dodged out of the kitchen and into the guest bedroom. Nothing I'd washed needed ironing, so I was able to get everything put away in a few minutes. I went down a mental checklist; I'd done everything for Marie I usually do on Tuesday mornings, and I'd be coming back again on Saturday. Marie was almost out of Glass Plus. In the kitchen, I left a note affixed to the refrigerator with an "I Heart Grandma" magnet. Marie gets money from Chuck to pay me, too; she'd write me a check on Saturday.

The police chief was gone when I emerged from the kitchen. I'd been waiting to hear the front door close behind him.

"Good-bye, Mrs. Hofstettler," I said. Marie was staring into space, her hands quiet in her lap. She seemed startled that I was still there.

"Good-bye, Lily," the old woman said wearily. "I'm so glad you came in today. This would have been hard to cope with on my own."

"Maybe you should give your son a call today."

"I hate to bother Chuck," Marie protested.

"This is a very awful thing that's happened." I remembered just how awful it had been in the narrow glow of my flashlight, in the dark, in the trees, in the middle of the night. But with a mental exercise as familiar as my bicep curls, I blocked it out. It would surface at another time and place, but by then I would be alone.

Tuesdays are always busy for me. Today was rougher than usual because I hadn't had enough sleep the night before and had endured great stress.

I ran in my house to grab some fruit to eat in the car on the way to my next job.

The garbage hadn't been picked up yet; Tuesday is also garbage day for my part of town. My cart was out in front, the garbage cans sitting in it correctly. No one could know or suspect that the garbage within those cans was double-bagged, that one set contained the traces of human remains. I had lifted the cans quickly that morning to see if any vestige of Pardon Albee's last ride was visible on the cart. To the naked eye, the metal looked quite clean.

As I went out the kitchen door to my carport, I could hear the rumble of the garbage truck coming. I couldn't resist standing there, one foot in the car and one arm propped on the open door, watching the truck approach. A middle-aged black man wearing a blue jumpsuit with "City of Shakespeare" stitched on the back hoisted out the garbage cans, one after another, dumped the bags into the back of the truck, and returned the garbage cans to the cart.

I closed my eyes in relief as the garbage truck moved up the street to the apartments. The clumsy vehicle turned cautiously to navigate the staple-shaped driveway. But it didn't idle long enough behind that building; I heard it moving again much sooner than it should have. I found myself wishing I could see through the privacy fence.

I was willing to bet that on the other side of it, policemen wearing rubber gloves were going through the apartment garbage cans.

It struck me as a sophisticated concept for the Shakespeare police force.

Though I had no way of finding out for sure, my guess was that the idea had originated with Chief Claude Friedrich.

I stood in the doorway of Bobo Winthrop's room and eyed it grimly. Bobo is a husky seventeen-year-old, full of hormones in overdrive, as I'd discovered last summer. He was at school today, but his room was evidence that Bobo had been home at least to sleep and change clothes often during the past week. There was furniture in the room, somewhere, under all the mess, and I remembered it was good furniture, just as Bobo, I had a gut feeling, was a good kid—under all the mess.

In other words, he didn't leave his room like this to spite me after I'd thumped him in the guts for putting his hand on my bottom. It's just that Bobo has been accustomed all his life to having someone clean up after him.

Days like this, I feel like I'm following an elephant in a parade, armed only with a puppy's pooper-scooper.

But since I am well paid by Beanie Winthrop to clean her house, I shouldn't grumble, I reminded myself sternly. Faced with Bobo's room, it was hard to remember why I'd chosen housecleaning as my means of support.

I was a National Merit Scholar, I reminded myself, dragging the plastic wash basket behind me as I worked my way across the room, tossing in soiled clothes as I went. I was top of my high school class. I finished college. My grade point average was 3.9.

On Tuesdays, that is my mantra.

Bobo had also ordered pizza one evening while his parents were out, I discovered. Probably—I evaluated by the layers of clothing over the cardboard box—about three days ago.

"Yoohoo!" came a light, sweet voice from the kitchen, accompanied by the slam of the door leading into the garage. "Lily! I'm just stopping by on my way to my tennis lesson!"

"Good afternoon," I called back, knowing my voice was (at best) grim. I much preferred seeing none of the Winthrops— not Beanie; her husband, Howell Junior; her oldest son, Bobo; or his younger siblings, Amber-Jean and Howell Three.

Beanie's maiden name had been, incredibly, Bobo: Beatrice ("Beanie") Bobo. The Bobos were sixth-generation Arkansas aristocrats, and I suspected Beanie had a slave-owning gene still in her DNA.

"Here I am, Lily!" Beanie cried with exaggerated joy, as though I had been on tenterhooks waiting for her appearance. And Beanie always makes appearances; she never just walks into a room. She popped into the doorway now like she was appearing in an English comedy: Attractive Lady Beatrice, on her way to play tennis, stops to speak to the parlor maid.

Beanie is undeniably attractive. She's in her middle forties, but her body doesn't know it. Though her face is not actually pretty, Beanie is a past mistress at maximizing what she has. Her long, thick hair is colored a discreet chestnut brown, her contacts make her brown eyes darker, and her tan is always touched up in the winter with a sun-bed session or two a week.

"Listen, Lily, wasn't that awful about Pardon?" Beanie was

in her chatty mode. "I went to high school with his little sister! Of course, even then Pardon wasn't the easiest person to get along with, but still . . . to be killed like that! Isn't it awful?"

"Yes."

"Ah . . . well, Lily, if you find Bobo's checkbook, please leave it on my desk. He hasn't balanced it in six months, and I promised him I'd do it. Though when he thinks I'll find the time, I don't know!"

"All right."

"Oh, and Lily—Bobo tells me you take karate. Can that be true?"

"Yes." I knew I was being uncooperative. I was in a bloody mood today. And I hated the idea of the Winthrops discussing me. Most days, I find Beanie amusing but tolerable, but today she was irritating beyond measure. And Beanie felt the same way about me.

"Well, now, we always wanted Bobo to take tae kwan do, but there never was anyone here to teach it, except that man who went broke after six months. Who do you take from?"

"Marshall Sedaka."

"Where does he teach it? At his gym?"

"He teaches goju karate to adults only on Monday, Wednesday, and Friday nights in the aerobics room at Body Time, seven-thirty to eight-thirty." Those three nights were the highlights of my week.

Beanie decided I was experiencing some kind of warming trend, and she beamed at me.

"So you don't think he'd teach Bobo? After all, Bobo's seventeen, and as much as I hate to admit it, he's practically an adult—physically, at least," Beanie added rather grimly.

"You can ask him," I replied. There wasn't a hope in hell

of Marshall taking on a spoiled kid like Bobo, but it wasn't my business to tell Beanie that.

"I just may do that," Beanie said, making a little note in the tiny spiral-bound notebook she keeps in her purse all the time. (That's something Beanie and Claude Friedrich have in common, I reflected.) And Beanie would call, too; one of the few things I find to admire about the woman is her devotion to her children. "Well," Beanie said dismissively, looking up and turning slightly as if she was already half out the door, "I'm just going to freshen up for a minute and then I'm off to the club. Don't forget about the checkbook, please!"

"I won't." I bent over to retrieve a sweatshirt Bobo had apparently used to clean his car's windshield.

"You know," Beanie said reflectively, "I think Pardon was that Marshall Sedaka's partner."

"What?" The sweatshirt slipped from my fingers; I groped around for it, hoping I hadn't heard correctly.

"Yes," said Beanie firmly. "That's right. Howell Junior told me, and I thought it was funny at the time, because Pardon was the most unfit man I've ever seen. He wouldn't walk down the street if he could ride. That gym's been a great success. It must have made Pardon a lot of money. Wonder who he left it all to?"

I just kept tossing clothes into the plastic wash basket. When I finally looked up, Beanie had gone, and a moment later I heard splashing noises from Beanie's big bathroom off the master bedroom.

After I heard the slam of the door to the garage, I said out loud, "I best start being nice to the mistress, else she sell me down the river." I really shouldn't be rude to her, I told myself seriously. Since they pay for me twice a week.

I go to Mrs. Hofstettler twice a week, too, but I charge her less—a lot less—because it takes me far less time and effort to straighten a two-bedroom apartment than it does the large Winthrop home, and also because the Winthrop children don't do the slightest thing to help themselves, at least as far as I can tell. If only they would put their own dirty clothes in the hamper and pick up their own rooms, they could save their parents quite a bit of my salary.

Normally, I am able to maintain my indifference to the Winthrops' personal habits, but this morning I was thrown off balance by what Beanie had said. Had Marshall and Pardon Albee really been in business together? Marshall had never mentioned a partner in the business he'd built up from scratch. Though Marshall and I knew each other's bodies with an odd, impersonal intimacy from working out at the same time and taking karate together, I realized we really knew little about each other's daily lives.

I wondered uneasily why I would worry about Marshall Sedaka, anyway. What difference would a partnership between Pardon and Marshall make? No matter how dim the light, I knew I'd have recognized Marshall if he'd been the person wheeling Pardon Albee's body into the park.

That realization made me feel even more uneasy.

Bending my mind ferociously to the job at hand, I found Bobo's errant checkbook and propped it on his mother's dressing table, where she'd be sure to spot it. Thinking was slowing me down; I still had to do Howell Three's room, and though he isn't the pig Bobo is, he isn't neat, either.

On my Tuesday at the Winthrops', I pick up, do the wash and put it away, and clean the bathrooms. On my Friday visit, I dust, vacuum, and mop. The Winthrops also have a cook, who takes care of the kitchen, or they'd have to hire me for a third time slot. Of course, on Fridays, too, I have to do a certain amount of picking up just to reach the surfaces of things I need to dust, and I get aggravated all over again at the people who are lazy enough to pay me to clean up their mess.

I soothed myself with a few deep breaths. Finally, I realized I was upset not because of the unthrifty Winthrops—their habits are to my benefit—or even because of Marshall Sedaka's possible involvement with Pardon Albee, but because right after I'd finished here, I had to meet with Claude Friedrich.

Three

He was exactly on time.

As I stepped back to let him in, I was again impressed by his size and presence.

The big thing about fear, I reminded myself, is not to show it. Having braced myself with that piece of personal junk philosophy, I found myself unable to show the policeman much of anything, besides a still face that could be construed as simply sullen.

I watched him scanning my sparse furniture, pieces that were on sale at the most expensive local stores, pieces I'd carefully selected and placed exactly where I wanted. It is a small living room, and I'd chosen with its size in mind: a reclining love seat with a footrest, rather than a sofa; a wing chair; small occasional tables; small pictures. I have a television set, but it, too, is not large. There are no photographs. There are library books, a large stack, on the bottom level of the table by my chair.

The prevailing colors in both upholstery and pictures are dark blue and tan.

"How long have you lived in this house?" Friedrich asked when he'd finished looking.

"I bought it four years ago."

"From Pardon Albee."

"Yes."

"And you bought it when you came to Shakespeare?"

"I rented it at first, with an option to buy."

"What exactly do you do for your living, Miss—is it Miss?—Bard?"

Titles are not important to me, nor is political correctness. I didn't tell him to call me Ms. But I saw that he had expected me to correct him.

"I clean houses."

"But a few things more than that?"

He'd done his research. Or maybe he'd always known about me, every detail of my life here in Shakespeare. After all, how much could the chief of police in this town have to occupy his mind?

"A few things." He required elaboration, his lifted eyebrows implying I was being churlish with my short answers. I suppose I was. I sighed. "I run errands for a few older people. I help families when they go out of town, if a neighbor can't. I get groceries in before the family comes home, feed the dog, mow the yard, and water the plants."

"How well did you know Pardon Albee?"

"I bought this house from him. I clean some apartments in the building he owned, but that is by arrangement with the individual tenants. I worked for him a couple of times. I saw him in passing."

"Did you have a social relationship with him, maybe?"

I flared up to speak before I realized I was being goaded. I shut my mouth again. I breathed deeply. "I did not have a so-cial relationship with Mr. Albee." As a matter of fact, I'd al-ways had a physical aversion to Pardon; he was white and soft and lumpy-looking, without any splendors of character to counterbalance this lack of fitness.

Friedrich studied his hands; he'd folded them together, fin-gers interlaced. He was leaning forward, his elbows resting on his thighs.

"About last night," he rumbled, shooting a sudden look over at me. I'd seated him on the love seat, while I was in the wing chair. I didn't nod; I didn't speak. I just waited.

"Did you see anything unusual?" He leaned back suddenly, looking straight at me.

"Unusual." I tried to look thoughtful, but felt I was prob-ably just succeeding in looking stubborn.

"I went to bed about eleven," I said hastily. I had—the first time, when I'd found I couldn't sleep. "Marie—Mrs. Hofstettler—told me this morning there was a lot of activity outside, but I'm afraid I didn't hear it."

"Someone called me about two-thirty in the morning," Friedrich said gently. "A woman. This woman said there was a body in the park, across the street from me."

"Oh?"

"Oh yes, Miss Bard. Now I think this woman saw some-thing, something about how that body got into that park, and I think that woman got scared, or knew who did it and was scared of that person, or maybe had a hand in Pardon Albee's turning up out there and just didn't want the poor man to lie in the park all night and get covered in dew this morning. So I think whoever it was, for whatever reason, had some concern about what happened to Pardon's remains. I sure would like to talk to that woman."

He waited.

I did my best to look blank.

He sighed, heavily and wearily.

"Okay, Miss Bard. You didn't see anything and you don't know anything. But if you think of something," he said with heavy irony in his voice, "call me day or night."

There was something so solid about Police Chief Claude Friedrich that I was actually tempted to confide in him. But I thought of my past, and of its emerging, ruining the sane and steady existence I'd created in this little town.

And at this moment, I knew the man was dangerous. I came out of my reverie, to find he was waiting for me to speak, that he knew I was contemplating telling him something.

"Good-bye," I said, and rose to show him to the door.

Friedrich looked disappointed as he left. But he said nothing, and those gray eyes, resting on me, did not look hostile.

After I'd locked the door behind him, I realized, apropos of nothing, that he was maybe the fifth person who'd entered my house in four years.

On Tuesday evenings at 5:30, I clean a dentist's office. When I first moved to Shakespeare and was living off my savings (what was left after I'd finished paying what the insurance didn't cover on my medical bills), while I built up my clientele, Dr. Sizemore had stayed until I got there, watched me clean, and locked the door behind me when I left. Now I have a key. I bring my own cleaning supplies to Dr. Sizemore's; he prefers it that way, so I charge him a little more. It is a matter of indifference to me whether I use my own supplies or the client's; I have my favorites, but they have theirs, too. I want to be Lily Bard who cleans; I don't want to be Busy Hands or Maids to Go or anything business-sounding.

Strictly privately, I call myself Shakespeare's Sanitary Service.

I'd thought of housecleaning as the ultimate in detachment when I'd decided how I would try to support myself, but cleaning has turned out to be an intimate occupation. Not only have I found out physical details about the people who employ me (for example, Dr. Sizemore is losing his hair and has problems with constipation) but I've learned more about their lives, involuntarily, than I feel comfortable with.

Sometimes I amuse myself by writing a fictional column for the biweekly *Shakespeare Journal* while I work. "Dr. John Sizemore recently received a bill from a skin magazine—and I don't mean the kind for dermatologists—so he's hiding the copies somewhere. . . . His receptionist, Mary Helen Hargreaves [when the locals said it, it sounded like Mare Heln] does her nails at work and reads English mystery novels on her lunch hour. . . . His nurse, Linda Gentry, finished a package of birth control pills today, so next cleaning night, there'll be Tampax in the bathroom."

But who would be interested in a column like that? The things I've learned are not things of real interest to anyone, though I was among the first to know that Jerri Sizemore wanted a divorce (the summons from the lawyer had been open on John Sizemore's desk), and I learned last week that Bobo Winthrop was practicing safe sex with someone while his parents were at the country club dance.

There are lots of things I know, and I've never told anyone

or even thought of it. But this thing I know, about the death of Pardon Albee . . . this, I thought, I might have to tell.

It would lead to exposure, I felt in my bones.

My life might not be much, but it's all I have and it's livable. I've tried other lives; this one suits me best.

I was through at Dr. Sizemore's at 7:30, and I locked the door carefully, then went home to eat a chicken breast, a roll, and some broccoli sprinkled with Parmesan cheese. After I'd cleaned up the kitchen, I fidgeted around the house, tried a library book, slammed it shut, and at last resorted to turning on the television.

I'd forgotten to check the time. I'd turned the TV on during the news. The pictures were among the worst: women holding screaming children, bombs exploding, bodies in the street in the limp grip of death. I saw the face of one desperate woman whose family was buried in rubble, and before my finger could punch the channel changer, tears were running down my face.

I haven't been able to watch the news in years.

Four

Wednesday mornings are flexible. It's the time I set aside for emergencies (special cleanings for ladies who are going to host the bridge club or give a baby shower) or rare cleanings, like helping a woman turn out her attic. This Wednesday, I had long been scheduled to help Alvah York with her spring cleaning. Alvah observes this rite even though she and her husband, T. L., live in one of Pardon Albee's apartments now that T. L. has retired from the post office.

Two years before, I'd helped Alvah spring-clean a three-bedroom house, and Alvah had started work before I arrived and kept on going at noon when I left. But Alvah has gone downhill sharply since the move, and she might actually need help for the two-bedroom apartment this year.

The Yorks' apartment is on the ground floor of the Garden Apartments, next to Marie Hofstettler's, and its front door is opposite the door of the apartment Pardon Albee kept for himself. I couldn't help glancing at it as I knocked. There was crime-scene tape across the door. I'd never seen any in real life; it was exactly like it was on television. Who was supposed to want to get into Pardon's apartment? Who would have had a key but Pardon? I supposed he had relatives in town that I didn't know of; everyone in Shakespeare is related in some way to at least a handful of the other inhabitants, with very few exceptions.

For that matter, how had he died? There'd been blood on his head, but I hadn't investigated further. The examination had been too disgusting and frightening alone in the park.

I glanced at my man-sized wristwatch. Eight on the dot; one of the primary virtues Alvah admires is punctuality.

Alvah looked dreadful when she answered the door.

"Are you all right?" I asked involuntarily.

Alvah's gray hair was matted, obviously uncombed and uncurled, and her slacks and shirt were a haphazard match.

"Yes, I'm all right," she said heavily. "Come on in. T. L. and I were just finishing breakfast."

Normally, the Yorks are up at 5:30 and have finished breakfast, dressed, and are taking a walk by 8:30.

"When did you get home?" I asked. I wasn't in the habit of asking questions, but I wanted to get some response from Alvah. Usually, after one of their trips out of town, Alvah can't wait to brag about her grandchildren and her daughter, and even from time to time that unimportant person, the father of those grandchildren and husband of that daughter, but today Alvah was just dragging into the living room ahead of me, in silence.

T. L., seated at their little dinette set, was more like his usual bluff self. T. L. is one of those people whose conversation is of 75 percent platitudes.

"Good morning, Lily! Pretty as ever, I see. It's going to be a beautiful day today."

But something was wrong with T. L., too. His usual patter was thudding, and there wasn't any spring in his movement as he rose from the little table. He was using his cane this morning, the fancy silver-headed one his daughter had given him for Christmas, and he was really leaning on it.

"Just let me go shave, ladies," he rumbled valiantly, "and then I'll leave the field to you."

Folding the paper beside his place at the table, he went down the hall. T. L. is a big, shrewd gray-haired man, running to fat now, but still strong from a lifetime of hard physical work. I watched T. L. duck into the bedroom doorway. Something else was different about him. After a moment, it came to me: This morning, he walked in silence. T. L. always whistles, usually country-and-western songs or hymns.

"Alvah, would you like me to come back some other time?"

Alvah seemed surprised I'd asked. "No, Lily, though it's right sweet of you to be concerned. I may as well get on with spring cleaning."

It looked to me as if it would be better for Alvah to go back to bed. But I began carrying the breakfast things into the kitchen, something I'd never had to do at the Yorks' before. Alvah had always done things like that herself.

Alvah didn't comment at all while I did the dishes, dried them, and put them away. She sat with her hands wrapped around a cup of coffee, staring into the dark fluid as if it would tell her the future. T. L. emerged from the bedroom, shaven and outwardly cheerful, but still not whistling. "I'm going to get a haircut, honey," he told his wife. "You and Lily don't work too hard." He gave her a kiss and was out the door.

I was wrong again in thinking Alvah would be galvanized

by her husband's departure. All she did was drink the coffee. I felt the skin on the back of my neck prickle with anxiety. I'd worked with Alvah side by side on many mornings, but the woman at the table seemed altogether different.

Alvah suffers from a pinched nerve in her back and is having increasing problems getting around, but she is normally a practical, good-natured woman with decided ideas about how she wants things done and a plain way of expressing them. She could offend by this straightforwardness, and I've seen it happen, but I've never minded her ways myself. There are few unexpressed thoughts hanging around in Alvah York's head, and very little tact, but Alvah is a good person, honest and generous.

Then I saw the supplies I'd brought in for the Yorks on Monday afternoon were exactly where I'd left them. The butter was in the refrigerator in the same place I'd laid it down, and the lettuce beside it hadn't been washed. At least the paper towels had been unwrapped, put on the dispenser, and used, and the bread had been put into the bread box.

I couldn't say anything more than I'd already said. Alvah wouldn't tell me what to do. So I mopped the kitchen.

Alvah has her own way of spring cleaning, and I thought I remembered she began by getting all the curtains down; in fact, the pair that hung in the living room on the window facing the street had already been removed, leaving the blinds looking curiously naked. So until very recently, Alvah had been operating normally. I cleaned the exposed blinds. They were dusty; Alvah had stopped just at that point, after she'd taken down the first pair of curtains.

"Is something wrong?" I asked reluctantly.

Alvah maintained her silence for so long that I began to

hope she wouldn't tell me whatever it was. But finally, she began speaking. "We didn't tell anyone around here," she said with a great weariness. "But that man over in Creek County—that Harley Don Murrell, the one who was sentenced for rape—well, that man . . . the girl he raped was our grandaughter Sarah."

I could feel the blood drain from my face.

"What happened?" I sat across from Alvah.

"Thank God they don't publish the victim's name in the paper or put it on the news," Alvah said. "She's not in the hospital anymore, but T. L. thinks maybe she should be—the mental hospital. She's just seventeen. And her husband ain't no help—he just acts mad that this happened to her. Said if she hadn't been wearing that leotard and tights, that man would have left her alone."

Alvah heaved a sigh, staring down at her coffee cup. She would have seen a different woman if she'd looked up, but I was hoping she wouldn't look up. I was keeping my eyes open very wide so they wouldn't overflow.

"But he wouldn't have," I said. "Left her alone."

Wrapped in her own misery, Alvah replied, "I know that, her mother knows that, and you know that. But men always wonder, and some women, too. You should have seen that woman Murrell's married to, her sitting up there in court when she should have been at home hiding her head in shame, acting like she didn't have any idea in the world what her husband was up to, telling the newspaper people that Sarah was . . . a bad girl, that everyone in Creek County knew it, that Sarah must have led him on. . . ."

Then Alvah cried.

"But he got convicted," I said.

"Yes," Alvah said. "He cried and screamed and said he'd got the Lord. It didn't do him a bit of good; he got convicted. But he'll get out, less someone kills him in prison, which is what I pray for, though the Lord may damn me for it. They say that other prisoners don't like rapists or child molesters. Maybe someone will kill him some night."

I recognized the tone, the words. I had to fight panic hard for a second. I was grateful for Alvah's absorption in her own troubles. My hand went up to my chest, touched the light yellow of my T-shirt, felt the ridges of the scars underneath it.

"Alvah, all I can do is clean," I said.

"Well, let's do that," Alvah said shakily. "We might as well."

For three hours, we worked in the small apartment, cleaning things that had never been dirty and straightening things that had never been messy. Alvah likes her life streamlined—she would live well on a boat, I've always thought. Everything superfluous was thrown away ruthlessly; everything else was arranged logically and compactly. I admire this, having tendencies that way myself, though I'm not as extreme as Alvah. For one thing, I reflected as I wiped the cabinets in the bathroom, Alvah has such limited interests that cleaning is one of her few outlets for self-expression. Alvah does a little embroidery of an uninspired kind, but she doesn't read or sew and is not particularly interested in cooking or television. So she cleans.

Alvah is a warning to me.

"What about the camper?" I asked when I thought we were almost through with the apartment.

"What?" Alvah said.

"We usually do the camper, too," I reminded her. The Yorks have a camper they pull behind their pickup truck, and when they visit their daughter, they park in her driveway and live in the camper. They can make their own coffee in the morning, go to bed when they feel like it, they've often told me. I'd been remembering while I worked how many times the Yorks had mentioned their grandaughter Sarah; youngest of their daughter's children, Sarah had been spoiled and had just last year made a bad marriage to a boy as young as she. But the Yorks have always doted on Sarah.

"You remember all the arguments Pardon gave us about that camper?" Alvah asked unexpectedly.

I did indeed. At each end of the residents' parking garage is a space about car width between the wall of the garage and the surrounding fence. The Yorks had asked permission to park their camper in the north space, and initially Pardon had agreed. But later, he'd reneged, insisting it stuck out and inconvenienced the other residents.

It had never been my business, so I'd paid little attention to the whole brouhaha. But I'd heard the Yorks carry on about it, and I'd seen Pardon standing out in the parking area, shaking his head at the camper as if it were a difficult child, puttering around it with a yardstick. Pardon Albee had been a fusser, a man apparently unable to let anything be.

He would never let a sleeping dog lie.

Now Alvah was weeping again. "You'd better go, Lily," she said. "This whole thing has just got me where I don't know if I'm going or coming. These past few days, when we were there for the trial, they have just been like hell. I'll do better next week."

"Sure, Alvah," I said. "Call me when you want to get your curtains back up, or if you want to clean the camper."

"I'll call you," Alvah promised. I didn't remind her that I

hadn't been paid; that was an indicator, too, since Alvah is always scrupulous about paying me on the dot.

I can always drop back by tomorrow, I thought. By then, perhaps some of the shock of Murrell's trial would have worn off.

Of course, Sarah's suffering would continue, for weeks and months and years. . . .

I realized it for sure wasn't my day as I was leaving the building. Deedra Dean came in the front door before I could get out of it.

I can't stand Deedra, especially since our conversation last week. We'd been standing right inside Deedra's upstairs apartment door. Deedra had come home for lunch and was ready to return to Shakespeare City Hall, where she almost earns a living as an office clerk.

"Hi, housekeeper!" Deedra had said chirpily. "Listen, I been meaning to tell you . . . last week I think you forgot to lock the door behind you when you left."

"No," I had said very firmly. Reliability is very important in my work, maybe even more important than doing an impeccable cleaning job. "I never forget. Maybe you did, but I didn't."

"But last Friday, when I came home, my door was unlocked," Deedra had insisted.

"I locked it as I left," I'd insisted right back. "Though," I'd added, struck by a sudden recollection, "Pardon was on his way up the stairs as I was coming down, and of course he has a master key."

"Why would he go into my apartment?" Deedra had asked, but not as if the idea was so ridiculous. As it sunk in even further, Deedra'd looked . . . well, a strange combination of angry and uneasy. I'd been intrigued by the sight of thought processes echoing through Deedra's empty head.

Deedra Dean, Deedra of the shiny blond hair, voluptuous figure, and a face completely undermined by its lack of chin. Deedra is always brightly made up and maniacally animated to distract the eye from that damning absence. Deedra moved into the apartment building three years ago and had screwed every male who had ever lived in the building, except (maybe) Pardon Albee and (almost certainly) T. L. York. Deedra's fond mother, a sweet, well-to-do widow who recently remarried, subsidizes Deedra heavily. Lacey Dean Knopp is apparently under the impression that Deedra is dating around until she finds Mr. Right. To Deedra, every man is apparently Mr. Right, for a night or two, anyway.

I've told myself often that it isn't any of my business, and I've wondered why Deedra's habits infuriate me. Gradually, I've come to the conclusion that Deedra's total lack of self-respect dismays me, Deedra's risk taking frightens me, and the ease with which Deedra has sex makes me envious.

But as long as I get paid on time by Deedra's mama, I keep reminding myself every ten minutes that Deedra is an adult, nominally at least, who can arrange her life as she chooses.

"Well, just don't let it happen again," Deedra had lectured me last week, with a lame attempt at sternness, after she'd accused me of leaving the door unlocked. Even Deedra's feeble brain had finally registered my anger. "Oh, gotta run! I had to come back to get my insurance card. I've got to get my car inspected on my lunch hour and get that tag renewal notice in the mail."

I'd wanted to say something to Deedra about her lifestyle,

something that would make a difference, but I knew nothing I could say would make an impression. And it was truly none of my business; Deedra was supposed to be grown-up. I'd watched out the window as Deedra hurried from the front door to her red sports car, left idling at the curb. Deedra's mother had made the down payment on that unreliable but flashy car; Deedra'd told me that quite casually.

"Did you ever find out if Pardon had been in your apartment?" I asked today. There was no one else in the ground-floor hall, and I kept my voice low. I had been following my own train of thought so intently, I'd forgotten that Deedra might be thinking of something quite different, and she looked at me now as if I was a very peculiar person.

"No," she said fiercely. I raised my eyebrows and waited. "And you better not tell the police you talked to me about that, either!"

"Oh?"

"You won't get any work in Shakespeare ever again," Deedra threatened. "I don't want to be involved in that old bastard getting killed."

"Do you seriously think," I said, one side of my mouth curling up in a very dry smile, "that anyone in this town would give up an excellent and reliable maid like me to protect your hide?"

Deedra's blue eyes widened in shock. A door opened on the second floor, and down the stairs came the Garden Apartments' only black tenant, Marcus Jefferson. Marcus, a handsome man in his late twenties, gave us a startled look, muttered a greeting, and pushed past us to the front door, which gave its heavy groan as it inched shut behind him.

This building was full of people behaving peculiarly today. When I looked back at Deedra, her face was brick red and she was watching the front door close on Marcus Jefferson.

Uh-oh. I had a flash of what might have finally prodded Pardon Albee into "doing something" about Deedra.

"Did you want me to come back on my regular day?" I asked. Perhaps Deedra didn't want my services anymore. I clean Deedra's apartment on Friday mornings. That is prime time, since everyone wants a house clean for the weekend, and I half-hoped Deedra would fire me.

"Oh . . . oh, yes. Listen, really, let's just forget all about that conversation we had last week, about the door. I left it unlocked, okay? I just remembered it later. I'm sorry I even thought you might have done it. You're just the most reliable . . ." Deedra's voice trailed off, a phony smile pasted to her face, where it looked quite at home.

As I walked down the sidewalk to my own house, I wondered if Pardon had indeed been in Deedra's apartment the week before. What would he go in there for? What would he have found if he did?

If he was looking for trash on how Deedra lived her private life, he'd have found plenty. In her top dresser drawer, Deedra keeps some pornographic pictures some lover had taken of her in exotic lingerie and some of her naked. I certainly hadn't wanted to know this little fact, but Deedra expects me to do her wash and put it away during the afternoon I spend cleaning the apartment, and that drawer is her lingerie drawer. Deedra also keeps some erotica and some ghastly magazines actually stuck under the bed (where I am obliged to vacuum), and of course the sheets are always a mess. There are probably other "incriminating" things there, too, things Deedra's mother might be interested to know about.

Would Pardon Albee actually have dared to call Deedra's mother, the very proper Lacey Dean Knopp?

By God, that would be just like him.

Five minutes after I had entered my own house, the doorbell rang. I checked my peephole and opened the door.

My visitor was surprising but nonthreatening—my seldom-seen neighbor, Carlton Cockroft. I've spoken to Carlton only three or four times a year since I bought the house.

There is something very "edible" about Carlton. He always reminds me of hot chocolate and caramels in the winter, or the coconut smell of tanning lotion and the tang of barbecue in the summer. Carlton is in his early thirties, like me. He has black hair and dark brown eyes, a cleft chin, and thick arched brows. He smells good. He is maybe four inches taller than I am, about five ten. My neighbor is polite, busy, and heterosexual—and that is the sum total of my knowledge.

"Hello, Lily," he said, his voice pleasant but not cheerful.

"Carlton." I nodded in greeting, then opened my door so he could step inside.

He looked very surprised, and I realized I'd never asked him in before. He looked at the room very quickly and didn't seem to know what to do with himself, quite unlike my assured visitor of the day before.

"Have a seat," I said, taking the wing chair.

"Lily, I'll come straight to the point," Carlton began after he'd settled himself on the love seat. He leaned forward, putting his elbows on his knees. He was wearing an unremarkable plaid shirt in navy blue and white, pleated blue jeans, and Reeboks; he looked informally prosperous and comfortable.

I waited for him to come straight to the point. Most people seem to think you should respond when they tell you they're about to do something, but I've always thought it more interesting to wait and see if they actually do it.

He kept his eyes on me for a moment, as if expecting something from me, sure enough.

I made an open-hands gesture—okay, the point?

"I saw you out walking the night of the murder." He waited for me to shriek in alarm. "I got up to get a sinus pill."

I shrugged. "So?"

"Lily, that puts you in a bad position. I didn't tell Friedrich, but he asked me an awful lot of questions about you. If anyone else saw you, I'm afraid he may even suspect you of having something to do with Pardon's death."

I thought for a moment, my hands folded on my lap.

"So, why are you here?" I asked.

"I just wanted to warn you," Carlton said, straightening from his intent-but-relaxed pose. "I've always worried about you some."

My eyebrows flew up.

"Yes, yes, I know," he said with a little smile. "None of my business. But you're a woman alone, a pretty woman, and since I live next to you I feel a little responsible . . . I sure don't want anything bad to happen to you."

I felt a terrible impulse to pull up my shirt and let him have a good look. The bad thing, the worst thing, had already happened to me. But I knew he was trying to shelter me, shield me from harm. I knew that Carlton perceived that as the right stance for a man to take. And I thought, as I so often do when dealing with them, that men are frequently more trouble than they're worth.

"Carlton, I live next to you, and since you're a good-looking guy living alone, I feel responsible for you," I said.

Carlton turned red. He started to get up, restrained himself. "I guess I deserved that. I should have turned it around in my own head to hear how it sounded, before it came out. But damnit, Lily, I'm trying to be your friend."

"I see that, Carlton, but why do you feel responsible for my possible trouble with the police? How do you know I'm not guilty of killing Pardon?"

My handsome neighbor looked at me as if I'd grown a snake's head and hissed. He was hurt, his gallant impulse rebuffed.

"Well . . ." he began stiffly, "well . . . I've just wasted my time. And yours."

I looked down at my right hand; my ring-finger nail had an aggravating notch in it. I'd have to get out my emery board before it got worse.

He said unbelievingly, "I'm trying to be nice to you."

I looked up at him steadily, debated whether or not to speak. "Carlton, you've dated too many women who thought you were just what they were looking for," I said.

I had observed the parade to and from his little house for four years. A good-looking guy with no visible vices and a steady income in a town this size? USDA prime.

"But thanks for not telling the police you saw me. As it happens, I don't know who killed Pardon, and I'd rather not spend a lot of time convincing the police of that."

I thought I'd been fairly agreeable. But Carlton said, "Goodbye, Lily," and stalked out in a huffy way. He remembered just in time not to slam the door behind him.

As I went to get my emery board, I shook my head. There was a good guy in there somewhere under a few layers of crusted manure. I wondered how Carlton had imagined his visit would go.

"Lily, I'm the handsome male next to you and I'm showing you by my silence that I'm gallant and dependable. You should develop a crush on me."

"Thank you, hunk who has never noticed me before. I was out late at night on a mysterious but innocent errand. I am truly not the peculiar person I sometimes seem, and I am so grateful you have shielded me from interrogation by the rough police. I am absolutely innocent of everything but a strong urge to go to bed with you and/or hire you to prepare my next tax statement."

I had a little laugh to myself, which was something I needed before I went to my next job.

The Shakespeare Combined Church secretary had called a few days before to ask me to serve and clean up after a board meeting for the SCC preschool, so I left home on foot at 4:55. After passing the apartment building, I began walking by the large parking lot, which is at the end of Track Street. The preschool building, which on Sundays houses the Sunday school, is set at the back of the parking lot and is one long two-story wing. An L-shaped covered walkway runs across the front of the preschool and up the side of the church proper, which faces Jamaica Street. The white-spired church is traditional red brick, but I know little about that part of the establishment. The offices of the minister and his secretary are on the second floor of the Sunday school wing.

If I ever resume going to church, my choice won't be Shakespeare Combined, or SCC, as the locals invariably call it. SCC was formed when lots of conservative splinter groups amazingly coalesced to combine incomes and hire a minister and build a facility that would serve them all.

They'd found the Reverend Joel McCorkindale and they'd fund-raised and collected until they'd had enough to build the church, then the Sunday school building. The Reverend McCorkindale is a super fund-raiser. I've seen him in action. He remembers *everyone's* name. He knows everyone's family connections, asks after ailments, condoles about losses, congratulates on successes. If he is ever at a loss, he humbly confesses it. He has a spanking-clean wife and two toothy, clean boys, and though I believe Joel McCorkindale truly loves his work, he makes the skin on my neck crawl.

I've learned not to ignore the skin on my neck.

As far as I know, Joel McCorkindale has never broken the law. Probably he never would. But I feel his potential to do something truly dreadful simmering right beneath the surface. I have lived one step away from losing my mind for years. I am quick and accurate in spotting unstable streaks in others.

So far, that strange streak has only shown itself in his hiring of the church janitor. Norvel Whitbread had shown up on the church doorstep one morning drunk as a skunk. Joel McCorkindale had taken Norvel in, given him a good dose of the Spirit (rather than spirits), and taken him on as church maintenance man. Like his boss, Norvel looks good on the outside; he is supposedly now sober, he has a genuine knack for fixing things, and he keeps a smile on his face for church members. He is voluble in his gratitude to the minister and the congregation, which makes everyone feel good.

Though Joel McCorkindale may have a dark monster inside, it may never surface; he's done a great job so far, keeping it contained and submerged. Norvel, however, is simply rotten inside, through and through. All his cheer is a sham, and I am sure his sobriety is, too. He is the most touched-up of whited sepulchres.

SCC pays Norvel's rent at the Shakespeare Garden Apartments, and a salary besides, and members of the church are always inviting him home to meals. In return, Norvel keeps the church bathrooms and the church floors clean, washes the windows twice a year, empties the garbage cans daily, picks up trash in the parking lot, and attempts minor repairs. He also does a little work for Pardon Albee at the apartments. But he won't do anything remotely domestic, like loading the huge church dishwasher or making and serving coffee. So I get the overrun of church duties, if none of the sisters of the church are available to serve for free.

This quarterly board meeting, comprising those elected to sit for staggered terms on the preschool governing board, is always a lively event, and I'm almost always hired to set up the coffee and cookie trays, because any sisters of the church overhearing this group would be liable to (depending on their individual temperaments) die laughing, or stomp out in exasperation.

Norvel Whitbread was lounging in the church kitchen, which is at the end of the preschool building farthest from the church, when I came in. A large broom and dustpan were leaning against the counter, establishing his bona fides.

"How're you [har yew] today, Sister Lily?" he drawled, sipping from a soft-drink can.

"I'm not your fucking sister, Norvel."

"You want this job, you better watch your mouth, woman."

"You want this job, you better stop spiking your Cokes."

I could smell the bourbon from four feet away. Norvel's thin, nose-dominated, undernourished face showed plain shock. I could tell it had been a while since someone had spoken to the church's pet convert in plain terms. Norvel was dressed in clothes passed on by a member of the congregation: the baggy brown pants and loose striped shirt had never been Norvel's choices.

While I got out the twenty-cup coffeepot, Norvel rallied.

"I'm a member of this church, and you ain't," he said, his voice low and mean. "They'll take my word."

"I'll tell you what, Norvel. You go on and tell them what you like. Either they'll believe you and fire me—in which case, the next woman they hire will be more than glad to tell them about your drinking habits—or they'll fire you, at the very least keep a closer eye on you. As I see it, Norvel, either way, you lose." My policy has always been to avoid or ignore Norvel, but today I was set on confronting him. Maybe my restraint with Carlton had worn out my quota of "nice" for the day; maybe this was just one face-to-face encounter too many. I often go for a week without talking to as many people as I'd talked to today.

Norvel struggled with his thought processes while I got the coffee apparatus assembled and perking and found a tray for the white-boxed assortment of bakery cookies that had been left on the counter.

"I'll get even with you for this, bitch," Norvel said, his

sunken cheeks looking even more concave under the merciless fluorescent lighting.

"No, you won't," I said with absolute certainty.

Inspired by the liquor or the devil or both, Norvel made his move. He grabbed his broom with both hands and tried to jab me with it. I grabbed the stretch of handle between his hands, ducked under his arm, twisted the broom, and bent. Norvel's arm was strained over the handle. It was excruciatingly painful, as I'd learned when Marshall taught me this particular maneuver, and Norvel made a high squeak like a bat's.

Of course, the Reverend Joel McCorkindale came in the kitchen right then. Before I saw him, I could tell who it was by the scent of his aftershave, for he was fond of smelling sweet. I slid my right foot behind Norvel's leg, raised it slightly, and kicked him in the back of the knee. He folded into a gasping mess on the clean kitchen floor.

I folded my arms across my chest and turned to face the minister.

Joel McCorkindale never looks like himself on the rare occasions when I see him with his mouth shut. Now his lips were compressed with distaste as he looked down at Norvel and back up at me. I figured that when he was an adolescent, McCorkindale had looked in the mirror and seen a totally forgettable male and then had vowed to become expert in using strength of personality and a remarkable voice to overcome his lack of physical distinction. He is of average height, weight, and unremarkable coloring. His build is average, neither very muscular nor very flabby. But he is an overwhelming man, able to fill a room with his pleasure, or calm, or conviction.

Now he filled it with irritation.

"What's going on here?" he asked, in the same marvelous voice God could have used from the burning bush—though I hoped God was above sounding peevish.

Norvel whimpered and clutched his arm. I knew he wouldn't try anything on me with his meal ticket standing there. I turned to the sink to wash my hands so I could return to arranging the cookies.

"Miss Bard!" boomed the voice.

I sighed and turned. Always, always, there was a payback time after I enjoyed myself.

People said so much they didn't need to say.

"What has happened here?" the Reverend McCorkindale asked sternly.

"Norvel got red-blooded, so I cooled him down."

This would require the least explanation, I figured.

And the minister instantly believed me, which I had figured, too. I'd seen him give me a thorough look once or twice. I'd had a strong hint he wouldn't find a man making a pass at me unbelievable.

"Norvel, is this true?"

Norvel saw the writing on the wall (so to speak) and nodded. I'd wondered if his shrewdness would overcome his anger.

"Brother Norvel, we'll have a talk later in my study, after the meeting."

Again, Norvel nodded.

"Now, let me help you up and out of here so Sister Lily can complete her work," said McCorkindale in that rich voice with its hypnotic cadence.

In a minute, I had the large kitchen to myself.

As I searched for napkins, I decided that Norvel's drinking

couldn't have escaped the overly observant Pardon Albee, since he saw Norvel at the apartments, too, as well as at church here. I wondered if Pardon had threatened Norvel with exposure, as I had done. Norvel would be a natural as Pardon's murderer. As a janitor, he might even be more likely to notice my cart as it sat by the curb on Tuesdays, and thus more likely to remember it when he needed to transport something bulky.

I grew fonder and fonder of that idea, without really believing it. Norvel is disgusting, and it would please me if he was gone from the apartments next door to my house. But I didn't really think Norvel had the planning ability to dispose of Pardon's body the way it had been done. Maybe desperation had sharpened his wits.

I put a bowl of artificial sweetener and a bowl of real sugar on the coffee tray. I got out two thermal coffee carafes and poured the perked coffee into them. By the time the board members had all assembled in the small meeting room right next to the fellowship hall, the cups, saucers, small plates, napkins, coffee carafes, and cookie trays had all been arranged on the serving table in the boardroom. I had only to wait until the meeting was over, usually in an hour and a half, to clean up the food things. Then I could go to my martial arts class.

For maybe a quarter of an hour, I straightened the kitchen. It was a good advertisement to do a little extra work and it kept me from being bored. Then I went out into the fellowship hall. The fellowship hall is about forty by twenty, and has tables set up all the way around the sides, with folding chairs pushed under them. The preschool uses the tables all week, and they get dirty, the chairs not evenly aligned, though the teachers carefully train the children to pick up after themselves. I neatened things to my satisfaction, and if I ended up close to the door where the meeting was taking place, well, I was bored. I told myself that like the things I happen to see in people's homes when I clean, the things I might happen to hear would never be told to another person.

The door to the meeting room had been left ajar to help the air circulation. This time of year, in a windowless room, the air tends to be close. Since I hadn't brought a book, this would help to amuse me till it was time to clean up.

One of the preschool teachers had mentioned evolution in her class during the course of Dinosaur Week, I gathered after a moment. I tried hard to imagine that as being important, but I just couldn't. However, the members of the board certainly thought it was just dreadful. I began wondering what enterprising child had turned in the teacher, what message it would send that child if the adult was fired. Brother McCorkindale, as they all addressed him, was for having the teacher in for a dialogue (his term) and proceeding from there; he felt strongly that the woman, whom he described as "God-fearing and dedicated to the children," should be given a chance to explain and repent.

Board member Lacey Dean Knopp, Deedra Dean's widowed and remarried mother, felt likewise, though she said sadly that just mentioning evolution had been a bad mistake on the teacher's part. The six other board members present were all for firing the woman summarily.

"If this is typical of the people we're hiring, we need to screen our employees more carefully," said a nasal female voice.

I recognized that voice: It belonged to Jenny O'Hagen, half of a husband-and-wife Yuppie team who managed the local outlet of a nationally franchised restaurant called Bippy's. Jenny and Tom O'Hagen manage to pack their lives so full of work, appointments, church functions, and phone calling connected to the various civic organizations they join (and they join any that will have them) that they've found a perfect way to avoid free time and conversation with each other.

Jenny and Tom live in the ground-floor front apartment at the Shakespeare Garden Apartments, the one right by Pardon Albee's. Naturally, they don't have a minute to clean their own apartment, so they are clients of mine. I'm always glad when neither one is home when I'm working. But most often, whichever one has been on the night shift is just getting up when I arrive.

I hadn't known the O'Hagens belonged to SCC, much less held a position on the board, but I might have figured. It was typical of the O'Hagen philosophy that childless Jenny had managed to finagle her way onto the preschool board, since the preschool is the most important one in Shakespeare and the waiting list for it is long. Jenny had probably made an appointment with Tom to conceive a child on October fifteenth, and was putting in her time on the board to ensure that infant a place in the preschool.

Since my clients were involved, I began listening with heightened attention to the heated words flying around the boardroom. Everyone got so excited, I wondered if I should have made decaf instead of regular coffee.

Finally, the board agreed to censure, not fire, the hapless young woman. I lost interest as the agenda moved to more mundane things like the church school's budget, the medical forms the children had to fill out . . . yawn. But then I was glad I hadn't drifted away to clean some more, because another name came up that I knew.

"Now I have to bring up an equally serious matter. And I

want to preface it by asking you tonight, in your prayers, to remember our sister Thea Sedaka, who's under a lot of strain at home right now."

There was dead silence in the boardroom as the members (and I) waited in breathless anticipation to find out what was happening in the Sedaka household. I felt a curious pang that something important had happened to Marshall and I was having to find out this way.

Brother McCorkindale certainly knew how to use his pauses to good effect. "Thea's husband is no longer—they have separated. Now, I'm telling you this very personal thing because I want you to take it into account when I tell you that Thea was accused by one of the mothers of one of the little girls in the preschool of slapping that child."

I sorted through the sentence to arrive at its gist. My eyebrows arched. Slapping children was a great taboo at this preschool—at any preschool, I hoped.

There was a communal gasp of dismay that I could hear clearly.

"That's much, much worse than mentioning evolution," Lacey Deene Knopp said sadly. "We just can't let that go, Joel."

"Of course not. The welfare of the children in our care has to be our prime concern," the Reverend McCorkindale said. Though he spoke as though he'd memorized a passage from the school manual, I thought he meant it. "But I have to tell you, fellow brothers and sisters in Christ, that Thea is deeply repentent of having even given the child cause to think she was slapping her."

"She denies it?" Jenny O'Hagen had thought that through before anyone else.

"What Thea says is that the child spoke back to her, not

for the first time, but for the seventh or eighth time in one morning. Now, Thea knows part of her job is to endure and correct behavior like that, but since she is under such a particular strain, she lost some of her self-control and tapped the child on the cheek to get her to pay attention. Like this, is how she showed me."

Of course, I couldn't see or hear the Reverend McCorkindale's demonstration.

"Were there any witnesses?" Jenny asked.

I decided Jenny had potential as an interrogator.

"No, unfortunately, Jenny. Thea and the child were alone in the room at the time. Thea had kept the child in from recess to discuss improving her behavior."

There was a silence while presumably the board members mulled this over.

"I think we have to call her on the carpet, Joel," rumbled the voice of one of the older men on the board. "Corporal punishment is a choice for the parents, not for the teachers at this school."

I nodded.

"So you want her to keep her job?" Joel McCorkindale inquired pointedly. "We have to reach a decision; she's waiting to hear. I must remind you that Thea is a steady churchgoer and she is in a very stressful situation. The parents of the little girl have said they would abide by our decision."

They practically begged McCorkindale to drive directly over to Thea's house and tell her all was forgiven—provided she didn't repeat the offense.

The minister didn't have any more bombshells to drop, and the meeting was clearly winding down. I took care to be out of sight in the kitchen when the board members emerged. It crossed my mind that Joel McCorkindale would come in the kitchen to ask more about my confrontation with Norvel, but after the board members had gone, I heard his steps ascend to his office on the second floor.

As I washed the dishes and sealed the plastic bags containing the leftover cookies, I found myself wishing that I'd stayed in the kitchen during the whole meeting. I would see Marshall Sedaka in minutes, and knowing something about his private life that he himself had not chosen to tell me made me uncomfortable. I glanced down at my big waterproof watch, then hurriedly wrung out the washcloth and folded it neatly over the sink divider. It was already 6:40.

Since I had only minutes to change into my gi, I was less than pleased to see Claude Friedrich leaning against his official car, apparently waiting for me. He'd pulled the car right up to the curb in front of my house. Was that supposed to fluster me?

"Hello, Miss Bard," he rumbled. His arms were crossed over his chest in a relaxed way. He was out of uniform, dressed casually in a green-and-brown-striped shirt and khakis.

"I'm in a real hurry now," I said, trying not to sound snappy, since that would imply he had succeeded in upsetting me.

"Isn't one of the advantages of a small town supposed to be the slower pace?" he asked lazily.

I stopped in my tracks. Something bad was coming.

"Shakespeare is quieter than, say, Memphis," he said.

I felt a sharp pain in my head. Though I knew it was emotional, it hurt as much as a migraine. Then I felt a wave of rage so strong that it kept me up straight.

"Don't you talk about that," I said, meaning it so much, my voice sounded strange. *"Don't bring it up."*

I went into my house without looking at him again, and I thought if he knocked on the door, he would have to arrest me, since I would do my best to hurt him badly. I leaned against the door, my heart pounding in my chest. I heard his car pull away. My hands were sweating. I had to wash them over and over before I pulled off my cleaning clothes and put on my spotless white gi pants. The top and belt were already rolled up in a little bag; I would just wear a white sleeveless T-shirt to Body Time and then put on the rest of my gi. I put my hand in the bag and touched the belt, the green belt that meant more to me than anything. Then I looked at the clock and went out the kitchen door to the carport.

I pulled into the Body Time parking lot just at 7:30, the latest I'd ever been. I pushed through the glass doors and hurried through the main room, the weights room. At this hour of the evening, only a few diehards were still working with the free weights or machines. I knew them enough to nod to.

I went quickly through the door at the back of the weights room, passing through a corridor along which doors lead to the office, the bathrooms, the massage room, the tanning-bed room, and a storage closet. At the end of the corridor are closed double doors, and I felt a pang of dismay. If the doors were closed, class had begun.

I turned the knob carefully, trying to be quiet. On the threshold, I bowed, my bag tucked under my arm. When I straightened, I saw the class was already in shiko dachi—legs spraddled, faces calm, arms crossed over their chests. A few eyes rolled in my direction. I went to one of the chairs by the wall, pulled off my shoes and socks, and faced the wall to finish putting on my gi, as was proper. I wound the obi around my waist and managed the knot in record time, then ran silently to my place in line, second. Raphael Roundtree and Janet Shook had unobtrusively shifted sideways to make room when they saw me enter, and I was grateful.

I bowed briefly to Marshall without meeting his eyes, then sank into position. After a few seconds of regulating my breathing, I peeked up at Marshall. He raised his dark eyebrows slightly. Marshall always makes the most of his quarter-Oriental heritage by working hard on inscrutability; his triangular face, its complexion somewhere between the pink of Caucasian and the ivory of Asian, remained calm. But the bird-wing eyebrows said volumes—surprise, disappointment, disapproval.

Shiko dachi is a position very like sitting on air, and it is painful and demanding even after long practice. The best way to get through it is to concentrate on something else, at least for me. But I was too upset to go into meditation. Instead, I scanned the line of fellow sufferers reflected in the mirror lining the opposite wall.

Newcomers are always at the end of the line. The newest man's head was bowed, his legs trembling—so probably the class had been in position for a minute and a half or two minutes. I hadn't missed much.

After a few seconds, I began to relax. The pain required my attention and the anxiety of my encounter with the policeman began to fade. I started my meditation on the kata we would practice later. Ignoring the ache in my quadriceps, I visualized the various moves that made up geiki sei ni bon, I reminded myself of mistakes I habitually made, and I anticipated further refining the grace and power of the kata, a series of martial arts strikes, blocks, and kicks woven together in what becomes almost a dance.

"Three minutes," said the first-in-line student, a huge black man named Raphael Roundtree. His watch was strapped to his obi.

"Another minute," said Marshall, and I could feel the dismay, though no one made a sound. "Be sure your thighs are parallel with the floor."

There was a general ripple of movement down the line as students corrected their stance. I stayed rock-still; my shiko dachi was as perfect as I could make it. My feet were the correct distance apart, pointing outward at the correct angle; my back was straight.

I emerged from my reverie for a moment to glance down the line in the mirror. The last-in-line man was in serious trouble. Though he was wearing shorts and a T-shirt, sweat was streaming down his face. His legs were trembling violently. With some amazement, I recognized my next-door neighbor, Carlton Cockroft, who had so generously let me know he'd seen me out walking in the night.

I shut my eyes and tried to refocus on the kata, but I was too full of surprise and conjecture.

When Raphael called, "Four minutes," it was as much relief to me as it was to the rest of the class.

We all stood, shifting from leg to leg to shake off the pain.

"Lily! Stretches!" Marshall said, his gaze just grazing me as it swept down the line. He retreated to a corner, where he watched us all for the slightest sign of slacking.

I bowed and ran to face the rest of the class. There were only eight that night. Janet and I were the only women, and we were much of an age, though I thought Janet might be thirty to my thirty-one. The men ranged from twenty to perhaps fifty-five.

"Kiotske!" I said sharply to bring them to attention. "Rai," I instructed, bowing to them. They bowed to me in return, Carlton only a beat behind. He was keeping a sharp eye on the man in line next to him, picking up on his cues. I wondered again why he was here. But the class was waiting for my directions, and I extended my right leg, balancing carefully on my left. "Big toe up . . . and down . . ." I said. A few minutes later, I was concluding with lunges to alternating sides, my hands extended to the front for balance.

I bowed to Marshall and ran back to my place.

"Teacher's pet," hissed Raphael out of the side of his mouth. "Late, too." Raphael and I pretty much alternate leading the stretches. Raphael is a high school math teacher, so I figure karate gives him a chance to blow off steam.

"First time," I whispered defensively, and saw his teeth flash in a grin.

Marshall told us to take a short break, and after a gulp of water from the fountain in the weights room, I strolled over to Carlton. He looked overdone, rather than edible. His face was red and his hair was wet with sweat. I'd never seen him approach tousled, much less disheveled.

Raphael drifted up behind me before I could say anything to my neighbor, and I introduced them. I consider Raphael a friend, although I never see him outside of class. Now I might get to know Carlton in the same way, after living next door to him for four years. He had apparently rethought something after our prickly conversation.

"So what made you decide to come to class, Carlton?" Raphael was asking with open curiosity. It was obvious Carlton was no workout buff.

"I keep Marshall's books," Carlton explained, which was

news to me. "And I've seen Lily heading out for class for four years now, since I bought the house next door to her. She always looks like she is happy to be going. I called Marshall today and he said to give it a shot. What comes next? I barely survived that shigga—whatever."

"Next," said Raphael, with an openly sadistic grin, "comes calisthenics."

"More?" Carlton was horrified.

I looked up at Raphael. We began laughing simultaneously.

I was still lacing up my shoes when the last class member left. I'd deliberately dawdled so I could talk to Marshall without asking him to preselect a time, which would have upset the balance of whatever relationship we have.

"Late tonight," Marshall commented, folding his gi top carefully and putting it in his gym bag. In his white T-shirt, his arms bare, the warm ivory tinge to his skin was more apparent. Marshall's grandmother had been Chinese and his grandfather American, he'd told Raphael in my hearing one night. Aside from his skin tone and his straight black hair and dark eyes, it would be hard to tell. He is a little older than I am—about thirty-five, I figure—and only three inches taller. But he is stronger and more dangerous than anyone I've met.

"Police," I said, by way of explanation.

"What—about Pardon?" Marshall gave me his attention.

I shrugged.

"Something was bothering you tonight," he said.

Marshall had never said anything more personal than "Good kick," or "Keep your hand and wrist in line with your arm," or "You've really worked on those biceps." Because of our long camaraderie, I felt obliged to answer.

"A couple of things," I said slowly. We were sitting on the floor about four feet apart. Marshall had one shoe on and was loosening the laces on the other, and he slipped it on and tied it while I was pulling on my second sock.

Marshall crossed his legs, wrapping them together in a yoga position, and pushed against the floor with his hands. He was suspended off the floor, his arms and hands taking all his weight. He "walked" over to me like that, and I tried to smile, but I was too uncomfortable with our new situation. We'd never had a personal conversation.

"So talk," he said.

I took as long as I could lacing up my shoe, trying to decide what to say. I looked over at him while he was distracted by the faint sound of the telephone ringing in his office. It cut off after the second ring; one of the employees had answered it.

Marshall's face is markedly triangular, with narrow lips and a nose that has been flattened a few times. He has a distinctly catlike look, but he doesn't have a cat's sleekness. He is built much more like a bulldog.

Well, I should either talk or tell him I'm not going to, I thought. He was waiting patiently, but he was waiting.

"Was Pardon Albee your partner?" I said finally.

"Yes."

"So what happens now?"

"We had a contract. If one of us died, the other got the whole business. Pardon didn't have anyone else to consider. I had Thea, but Pardon didn't want to deal with her. So he carried a heavy insurance policy on me, and Thea would get that money if anything happened to me, instead of getting a share of the business."

"So . . . you own Body Time now."

He nodded. His eyes were fixed on me. I was used to being on the dispensing, rather than the receiving, end of fixed stares, and it was an effort not to fidget. Also, Marshall was a good bit closer to me than people were in the habit of getting.

"That's good," I said, with an effort.

He nodded again.

"Have the police talked to you yet about Pardon?" I asked him.

"I'm going to go talk to Dolph Stafford tomorrow at the police station. I didn't want them to come here."

"Sure." I thought I could hardly bring up Thea; Thea's slapping the little girl was something I wasn't supposed to know, though if I knew the Shakespeare grapevine, everyone in town was hearing some version of the incident by now. And I couldn't just blurt out a question as to why Marshall and Thea had separated.

The air was getting pretty thick with something, and I was feeling increasingly nervous.

"So . . . the other thing?" he asked quietly.

I glanced over at him quickly, then back down at my hands, fidgeting with the damn shoelaces. "Nothing else I can talk about," I said dismissively.

"I've left Thea."

"Oh."

We stared at each other a little more, and I felt a bubble of hysterical laughter rising in my throat.

"Don't you want to know why?"

"What? Why what?" I knew I sounded stupid, but I just couldn't seem to concentrate. It was taking an effort to keep still. A private conversation, physical closeness, personal talk— these are unnerving things.

Marshall shook his head. "Nothing, Lily. Can I ask you something in return?"

I nodded rather warily. I wondered if we looked like two of those wooden birds on the stand, bobbing at each other.

"Where'd you get the scars?" he asked gently.

Five

The room was suddenly airless.

"You don't really want to know," I said.

"Of course I do," Marshall said. "We're never moving beyond where we are now unless I know that."

I looked at the mirror beyond Marshall's shoulder. I saw someone I didn't recognize.

"People never feel the same about me once they know," I said. My mouth was suddenly so dry, it was hard to speak.

"I will," he said.

He wouldn't. It would ruin the unspoken bond between us—a bond with which, evidently, he was no longer content.

"Why do you want me to talk about it?" My hands were clenched and I could see them shake.

"I can never get to know you better until I know that," he said with patient certainty. "And I want to get to know you better."

With one quick movement, I jerked off my T-shirt. Under it, I was wearing a plain white sports bra. Marshall's breath hissed as he got a good look at the scars. Not meeting his eyes,

I turned a little so he could see the ones that crossed my shoulders like extra bra straps; I rotated back to show him the ones that striped my upper chest; I sat up straight so he could see more thin white scars in an arc pattern descending into the waistband of my pants.

And then I looked him in the eyes.

He did not blink. His jaw was fixed in a hard line. He was making a heroic struggle to keep his face still.

"I felt them when I gripped your shoulders in class last week, but I didn't know they were so . . ."

"Extensive?" I asked savagely. I would not let him look away.

"Are your breasts cut, too?" he asked, with a creditable attempt at keeping his voice neutral.

"No. But all around. In *circles*. In a *pattern*."

"Who did this?"

What had happened to me had cut my life in two, more deeply and surely than the knives that had traced bloody festoons on my skin. Unable to stop, I remembered once again, descending into a familiar hell. It had been hot that June. . . .

It had already been hot for a month. I had graduated from college and had been living in Memphis for three years. I had a nice apartment in east Memphis and a desk job at the city's largest maid and janitorial service, Queen of Clean. In spite of the stupid name, it was a good place to work. I was a scheduler. I also did spot checks on site and made courtesy calls to customers to see if they were satisfied. I earned a descent salary, and I bought a lot of clothes.

When I left work that Tuesday in June, I was wearing a

short-sleeved navy blue dress with big white buttons down the front and white leather pumps. My hair was long and light brown then, and I prided myself on my long, polished fingernails. I was dating one of the co-owners of a bottled-water supply company.

My worst problem was the transmission of my car, which had already required extensive repairs. When I left work, I began to worry that it was going to eat up more of my money.

The car made it down the freeway to the Goodwill Road exit before I had to stop. There was a service station in sight on Goodwill, and lots of traffic, people everywhere. I walked down the exit ramp, nervous about how narrow it seemed when it had to accommodate a woman on foot and cars. Unexpectedly, a van coming slowly down the ramp stopped beside me. I thought, They're going to offer me a ride to the service station.

The passenger door was thrown open by someone sitting in the back, who immediately retracted into his crouch behind the passenger's seat. The man in the driver's seat was holding a gun.

When I accepted it for what it was, rather than trying to imagine it was something else, my heart began racing, its thud so loud, I could hardly make out what he was saying.

"Get in or I'll shoot you where you stand."

I could jump off the exit ramp and get hit by a car speeding on the road below, or I could tell him to shoot, or I could get in the van.

I made the wrong decision. I got in.

The man who had picked me up, I found out later, was an accomplished kidnapper named Louis Ferrier, called "Nap" by his customers in acknowledgment of his expertise in stealing women and children, most of whom vanished forever. The abducted victims who did resurface were without exception dead, either mentally or physically. Nap had done jail time, but not for his specialty.

I was handcuffed the minute I got in the van by the man crouched behind the passenger's seat, an occasional accomplice of Nap's named Harry Wheeler. Harry reached around the seat, grabbed my hands, cuffed them, and held the chain that led from the cuffs. Then he blindfolded me. The windows of the van were heavily tinted. No one noticed.

During that dreadful ride out of Memphis, they just talked as if I wasn't there. I was in such a state of terror, I hardly knew what they said. I could feel death sitting in my lap.

At the end of the ride, which had led north from Memphis, Nap and Harry exited the highway and met with a representative of a biker gang at a prearranged rendezvous. Nap had rented me to the gang for one night, though I didn't know that.

Four men and one woman took me to an abandoned shack in the middle of some fields. One of the men had grown up around there and was familiar with the place. They attached the chain through my handcuffs to the metal head rail of an old cot. I was still blindfolded. The men drank, ate, and raped me. When that got old, they used the knife on my chest. They cut a circle around the base of each breast. They cut zigzags in the flesh covering my chest. They cut a target on my stomach, with my navel as the bull's-eye. They laughed as they did this, and I, chained to a dilapidated bed, screamed and screamed, until they slapped me and told me to stop or the knife would go deeper. And they raped me again.

The woman said very little during all this. I refused to

believe, at first, that a woman could be present and not help me. When I realized the softer voice did indeed belong to a woman, I pleaded with her and begged her for help. I got no reply, but during a time when the men all seemed to be sleeping or outside urinating, the woman's voice came close to my ear and said, "I lived through it. You can, too. They're not cutting you bad. You haven't lost anything but a little blood."

I had not known that Nap was supposed to return for me, that I had been rented, not sold. I expected to die when the men tired of me and were ready to leave; I had had eighteen hours to anticipate my death.

I'd attached the name Rooster to the largest man. Rooster had a wonderful idea as they packed up their gear the next day. He had a cheap little revolver he'd picked up on the street, and he left it with me. He also left me one bullet.

"Now, you can use this on yourself," he said genially. "Or you can save it for Nap, when he comes back to get you, and use it on him. I figure it'll take you from now till he gets here to learn how to use it."

"Be better if we killed her ourselves," said a voice I hadn't attached to a name or weight.

"But look at it this way," urged Rooster. "If she kills Nap, we can always say she wanted to have sex with us, if worse comes to worse and somehow she finds us, though that ain't likely. But if we kill her, Nap'll come after us when we least expect it. Ain't you kind of sick of him? I know I am."

This made good sense to the rest. Leaving me with a gun appealed to their sense of humor, too. As they left, they were laughing over Nap's surprise, and placing bets over whether or not I would choose to kill him or myself.

For some minutes after I heard the motorcycles buzz down

the dirt road to rejoin the blacktop, I lay in a stupor. I could not believe I was still alive. I didn't know if I was glad or not. I wondered how long I would survive, with the wounds I had. My vaginal area was at best badly bruised; at worst, I had internal rips. I was oozing blood from the cutting, and the pain was dreadful, though I knew the cuts were not deep.

Very gradually, I realized I really was still alive, still alone, and the sense of what Rooster had said began to filter in. I raised my cuffed hands and worked off the blindfold.

The man who had kidnapped me was coming to retrieve me, to rent me out again for more of the same.

I had a gun and one bullet. It was so tempting, the thought of being out of all this. But what stopped me was the thought of my parents. They would know by now I was gone; people would be looking for me. I might not be found for years out here in this shack, and in all that time they would worry about me, pray for me, refuse to believe I was dead.

It suited me better to kill the man they called Nap. After a moment, I began to look forward to it.

Every moment cost me pain, but I figured out how to load the revolver, though the handcuffs made it difficult; at least there was enough slack in the chain to move my arms. I loaded, emptied out the bullet, and reloaded several times, until I had mastered it and knew the bullet was in the chamber that would fire. Then I tucked the gun down by my side and waited in the stinking, hot shack for Nap to come for me. I could see the sky through a hole in the roof; when the sun was almost overhead, I heard a van coming down the dirt road. I remembered the second man, and prayed he hadn't come this time.

I shut my eyes when the footsteps came close.

"How you feeling this morning, honey?" Nap asked jovially. "Where did Rooster leave that key? Shit, they messed you up. It's gonna take you a while to get over this. . . ." I could tell he was angry that I was too damaged to be useful for a while. I opened my eyes and looked at him, straight at him, and what he saw made him stop in the act of picking up my discarded blindfold.

I raised the gun and pointed it as carefully as I could, then fired.

It caught Nap in the eye.

He died far too quickly to suit me.

Of course, I had no idea where the key to the handcuffs was. Nap had said he'd left it with Rooster. I slid off the cot, then hitched myself across the floor, dragging the cot behind me. With incredible difficulty, I searched Nap just to make sure it wasn't on him. It wasn't.

It seemed to me there must be a way I could get out of the shack, but trying to get myself and the cot through the door was too hard for me. By that time, I was weak.

So I got to lie on the bed in the shack with the dead man for another day. Bugs came, and my cuts got infected, and the body began to smell.

By the time a farmer working in the adjacent field came to investigate Nap's van, maybe twenty-four hours later, I was running a high temperature, but not high enough to make me delirious. I longed for unconsciousness the way people in hell want ice water. The farmer saw the body of Nap lying on the floor inside the open door and ran to call for help. The flood of people who arrived after that had no idea a live person was inside the shack. The horror on the faces of the men who came to investigate the body told me that I had gone beyond some boundary.

I had passed; I had become the thing that had happened to me.

No one who saw me chained to that bed would ever be able to imagine that I'd had a dog named Bolo when I was little, that I'd enjoyed playing with dolls, that I'd gotten three raises in the past two years, that I came from a home as clean and orderly as any of theirs.

In the slow weeks of recovery, after repeated questioning by law-enforcement officials on several levels, after enduring a media drench that sensationalized what was already sensational, I realized that returning to my former life was no longer possible. It had been stolen from me. My boyfriend was still posing for the newspapers as my boyfriend, but he wasn't any longer. My parents simply could not cope with the horror of my ordeal or my execution of the man responsible.

I began to suspect that, in their secret hearts, they thought I had made the wrong choice in my use of the bullet.

My younger sister, Varena, was a rock at first, but gradually my slow physical and mental recovery wore Varena's lighthearted nature down and then defeated it. Varena was ready for me to rise from my bed and walk. Varena was ready to refer to my crisis in the past tense, to have conversations that did not refer to it even in terms of my recovery. After a few increasingly acrimonious exchanges that included such statements as "Pull up your socks and get on with your life" and "You can't go on living in the past," Varena drifted back to her normal routine of nurse's duties at the little hospital in our family's town, teaching Sunday school, and dating a local pharmacist.

For a month longer, I stayed with my parents, with my belongings stored in their attic and toolshed. There was a healing quality in the house with the big front porch and the rose garden, the known neighbors. But most of those neighbors found it impossible to be natural around me; the best managed it, but the sheer horror of my victimization defeated the rest.

I tried hard not to be a tragic figure, tried desperately to reclaim my past, but I finally acknowledged defeat. I had to leave Bartley, to forget Memphis, to go somewhere new.

"**And why did you** pick Shakespeare?" Marshall asked me.

"The name," I said, almost surprised that someone else was with me. I pulled my T-shirt back over my head. "My name is Bard, as in the Bard of Avon. This is Shakespeare."

"You just picked it off the map like that?"

I nodded, stood. "I'd tried a couple of places earlier that didn't work out, so random selection seemed as good a method as any." I stood still for a moment. It was such an effort to move.

"I'll see you later," I said. "I don't want to talk any more now." I lifted the bag with my gi and obi inside and strode out, not forgetting to turn and bow as I reached the door.

I drove home automatically, trying to keep my mind blank. It had been years since I had told my story, years since I had relived it in full. They had been good years, having people look at me quite normally, as if I was a full woman, not a thing, not a victim.

Now Chief Friedrich had indicated he knew who I was, so he knew I'd killed someone. Maybe he'd think I had had some kind of flashback and killed Pardon Albee, too. The pointed question about a personal relationship might mean that he suspected I'd killed Pardon because he'd paid me unwelcome attention. Knowing Pardon, that was a strange idea.

I sat on the side of my bed when I got home. I tried to picture myself as a vigilante, as some kind of—who was the girl who'd been raped in *Titus Andronicus*? Lavinia . . . yes, Lavinia, whose hands and tongue had been cut out by her attackers so that she could not reveal their identity. But Lavinia, I remembered, managed to tell her brothers somehow, and served the attackers to their mother as lunch, since the mother had permitted the rape to happen.

I wasn't set on gaining some kind of vengeance on all men for what had happened to me. But I certainly wasn't a trusting person anymore, and I definitely never expected much of people, and I would never be surprised to hear of any perfidy again.

I did not believe in the underlying goodwill of men or the unspoken sisterhood of women.

I did not believe that people everywhere are really the same, or that if you treat people kindly you will get kindness in return.

I did not believe in the sanctity of life.

If all the men were lined up in front of me, the four rapists and the man who cuffed me, and I had a loaded gun . . . I would kill them all, I thought. But I'm not scouring biker bars across America and I'm not standing in post offices looking at wanted posters to see if they've done anything else. I haven't hired a private investigator to look for them.

Did that speak to my sanity, or did that say I would commit murder only if it was convenient? I felt a tingling all over, like a hand that had been asleep prickling as it woke up. I'd felt that before after the times when I couldn't dodge remembering. It was the rest of my personality seeping back into the shell I became when I immersed in the memory.

I turned down my covers, checked that my alarm clock was set, and gratefully crawled into bed. I reached over to switch out the lamp.

I'd kill the woman, too, I thought, feeling a wave of weariness sweep through my body. The woman I'd never seen. The bikers I'd never actually seen, only heard, felt.

But Pardon Albee—could Friedrich really believe I'd kill someone like that, someone I knew in the ordinary course of my life?

Of course he could.

I wondered what weapon had been used to kill the landlord. I hadn't seen much blood, though I hadn't examined Pardon very carefully. Since I'd been taking Goju from Marshall for two years or more, I thought maybe I could kill someone with my hands if I needed to—that had originally been my reason for studying a martial art.

That, too, would enter Friedrich's picture of me: a very fit woman . . . in conjunction with a middle-aged, nosy, presumably heterosexual man who lived very close to me. . . . Put like that, it seemed pretty obvious to me that I must have killed Pardon in my sleep.

Starting tomorrow, I decided as I rolled onto my left side, I have to find out who killed the landlord. In the stage before sleep, it seemed that simple.

Six

I was on my way into the house to shower after my morning workout at Body Time—Marshall's assistant had opened the gym this morning, to my relief—when I saw Marcus Jefferson and a little boy. My hair was wet with sweat and big dark patches spotted my gray T-shirt and shorts. I was about to unlock my front door when I heard someone call my name.

"Good morning, Lily," Marcus said from the sidewalk. It was the first time I had ever seen him smile, and I understood the attraction he has for Deedra. Marcus is well-muscled and tall, the color of coffee with one tablespoon of milk. His brown eyes have a golden cast. The little boy looked even more attractive, smiling and immaculately dressed, with long, curly eyelashes and huge dark eyes.

Though I longed to go right inside and get in the shower, out of courtesy I strolled down my driveway to the sidewalk and squatted down in front of the child.

"What's your name?"

"Kenya," the boy said with a beaming grin.

"Kenya, that's a nice name," I said. "How old are you?" I supposed I was asking the right questions, since Marcus and the child both seemed pleased.

The boy held up three fingers. I had to repress a shudder at seeing how tiny those fingers were. The terrible vulnerability of children frightens me so much, I am leery of liking one. How could I ever be vigilant enough to protect something so frail and precious? Yet other people don't seem to share this terror, are foolish or defiant enough to have children and expect those children will live to adulthood without being harmed.

My face had gone wrong, I could tell. The child's uncertain eyes and faltering smile recalled me to my senses.

I yanked my lips into a grin and very gently patted the boy's shoulder. "You'll grow up to be a big man, Kenya," I said, and rose to my feet. "Is this your son, Marcus?"

"Yes, this is my only one," he said proudly. "My wife and I have been separated for a few months, but she and I agree that I should spend as much time with Kenya as I can."

"You must have worked four to midnight," I said, pretty much at a loss for conversation topics.

Marcus nodded. "I came home and got some sleep; then I got Kenya from his mom before she left for work—she works at the welfare office."

"So, what are you two going to do today?" I asked politely, trying not to look at my watch. Thursday mornings, I have to be at the Drinkwaters' at 8:30.

"Well, we're going to McDonald's for breakfast," said Marcus, "and then I think we'll go to my place and play Candy Land, and maybe we'll watch Barney. That suit you, sport?"

"McDonald's, McDonald's," Kenya began to chant, pulling on his father's hand.

"I better take this boy to get some food in him," Marcus said, shaking his head at the boy's impatience. But he was grinning at the same time.

"I guess," I said, "you couldn't have him here, with Pardon being the way he was about the apartments being adults only."

"I had Kenya over one time, and Mr. Albee let me have it," Marcus said, watching the child trot down the sidewalk. "I'm wondering what the next owner will do. Would you know who that's going to be?"

"No," I said slowly. This was the second time the subject had come up. "No, I have no idea. But I'm going to try to find out."

"Let me know," Marcus said, and raised a hand in good-bye.

"Cute kid," I said, and watched the young man trot to catch up with the little boy before I turned to go into my own house.

Mel and Helen Drinkwater have me in once a week for an all-morning cleaning job. They are both in their fifties and work, he as county supervisor, she at a bank, and they are not messy people. But they have a large old house and their grandchildren, who live down the street, come in and out several times a week.

Helen Drinkwater is a woman who likes things done exactly to her taste, and she has a room-by-room checklist of things I should accomplish in the three and a half hours I am there. At first, Mrs. Drinkwater actually tried to get me to check things off the list and leave a checked list in each room, but I wouldn't. In fact, as I was learning the Drinkwater house, the list was helpful, but it would have felt like a paint-by-numbers kit if I'd checked the little boxes.

Mrs. Drinkwater (I have sworn never to call her Helen) hadn't said a thing. I'd left the list in the exact middle of the room each time I'd cleaned the house the first few visits.

Then Mrs. Drinkwater had left a pile of dirty clothes by the washer with a note asking me to "pop these in the washer and dryer for me." The first time it happened, I had fumed and done it; the second time, I left a note myself, which said, "Not on any of my lists," and after that, Helen Drinkwater had not added to my duties.

The two-story turn-of-the-century family home looked especially pretty in the clear, warm morning light. The house is pale yellow, with white trim and dark green shutters, and it is set far back from the street. Of course, a house like this is in the oldest surviving section of Shakespeare, and it has at least half an acre of woods behind it, which the Drinkwaters have left untouched.

This morning, I had a lot to think about. Marshall had said he was separated from Thea, and he'd said it as if that was significant to me. As I scrubbed the second-floor bathroom, I wondered if Marshall still had that spark of feeling for me after last night. The few times in the past I'd felt more than calm acceptance of a man, all I'd had to do to make him run was to tell him what had happened to me. Except one man, who'd gotten so excited that he'd tried to force himself on me. I'd hurt him, but it had taken time and a struggle. After that, I'd been ready to try martial arts, which has turned out to be the most pleasurable element in my life.

These thoughts tapped at my consciousness like raindrops hitting the sidewalk, thoughts that were significant but not wholly engrossing. I was also thinking about the Drinkwaters' bathtub ring, and what to do with the comic book I'd found behind the toilet. So it wasn't until the floorboards downstairs creaked a second time that I came to attention.

I became absolutely still, the sponge in my hand held motionless an inch from the surface of the sink. I was looking into the mirror over the sink, but I was not seeing myself. I was trying to make sense of the floorboards.

The Drinkwaters always leave the kitchen door unlocked when they depart at 8:15, knowing I will be here at 8:30. I lock it behind myself when I get here, though daytime burglaries are unknown in this section of Shakespeare.

Someone had gotten in the house in that fifteen minutes.

I shut my eyes to listen harder. I tried to pull off my rubber gloves without making a sound. I set them in the sink. He'd not yet started up the stairs; I could improve my position.

There wasn't time to take off my shoes. I stepped silently out of the bathroom, trying to remember where the creaking boards upstairs were. If I could flatten myself against the wall at the beginning of the hall, which leads off at right angles from the stairs, I would be ready to strike when the intruder reached the top.

I crept closer to the stairs, flexing my hands to loosen the muscles. My heart had begun pounding heavily, and I felt a little light-headed, but I was ready—I would not be afraid; I would fight.

I should relax; I felt the tightness of my muscles; it would slow me down . . . so many things to think of.

He was on the stairs.

My hands clenched into fists and my leg muscles were hard and tense. My blood pounded harder through my heart.

A little noise, like material brushing against the wall. Very close.

Then there was a tiny sound I couldn't interpret. I felt a frown pull my brows together.

Had it been something metal?

And another creak of the stairs.

Surely—the creak had been from a lower step?

I shook my head, puzzled.

The next sound was from even farther, off the steps entirely, all the way into the kitchen. . . .

Getting *away,* the son of a bitch was getting away!

I flew down the stairs, ignoring something white as I pelted down, rage lifting me out of myself so that I barely felt my feet touch the floor. But I heard the slam of the back door as I came through the kitchen doorway, and though I was only seconds behind him, it was enough for the intruder to conceal himself in the woods in back of the Drinkwaters' house.

I stood in the door for a minute or more, panting. For the first time, I understood the phrase "spoiling for a fight." Then common sense prevailed and I retreated, locking the kitchen door behind me.

I suffered an immediate reaction to the adrenaline my body had pumped into my blood to prepare me for action; at every step, I felt my flesh sag on my bones. With a terrible reluctance, I went to see what had been left on the stairs. A spotless white handkerchief was tented over something about halfway up. I reached out slowly and pulled off the handkerchief.

Shining in the sun pouring through the stained-glass window at the landing was a set of cheap metal toy handcuffs. By them was a plastic gun.

I sank onto the stairs and buried my head in my hands.

Three days ago, my past life had been a secret, or so I'd thought.

Now Claude Friedrich knew about my misfortunes. I'd told Marshall. Who else knew?

The life I had so carefully constructed was falling apart. I tried to find something to hold on to.

And I recognized, once again, the bleak truth: There was nothing but myself.

I searched the house. I talked to myself the whole time, telling myself that after it was searched and safe, I would finish cleaning it, and I did. It was a tremendous relief to leave the house and return to my own. I called Helen Drinkwater at work and told her that on my drive to work, I'd seen a suspicious man at the edge of the yard.

"I think you shouldn't leave it unlocked even for the fifteen minutes before I come," I said. "So either I have to get there while you're there, or you need to give me a key." I could feel the woman's suspicions coming over the phone line, along with a tapping sound. Helen Drinkwater was tapping her teeth with a pencil. Mrs. Drinkwater doesn't actually like to see me; she just likes to enjoy the results of my having been there. Before this morning, that had suited me just fine.

"I guess," she said finally, "you better come earlier, Lily. You can just wait in the kitchen until we leave."

"I'll do that," I said, and hung up.

The vicious game played with me today would not be repeated. I lay down on my bed and thought about the incident. It could be that the intruder had not known I could hear the little sound of the boards creaking; perhaps he'd just anticipated that I'd start down the stairs at some later time and find the cuffs and gun. Of course the intruder hadn't planned on any kind of confrontation; that was plain from the way he'd rabbited out the back door. But somehow, it made a difference whether or not the intruder had intended me to be aware of his presence before he left the house.

I would have to think about it. Maybe ask Marshall.

And that brought me upright on the bed instantly. I slapped myself on the cheek.

Marshall was on the edges of my life; he had probably left it completely after our conversation the night before. I won't start to think of him as part of my life, I promised myself. He'll go back to Thea. Or he's completely gone off me, since I told him about the scars. Or his common sense will tell him he doesn't need someone like me.

After that, I swore off thought for the day. I ate a hasty sandwich, then left the house.

I have two clients on Thursday afternoons, and I felt it had been a very long day when I left the last one, a travel agent's office, at 6:30. The last thing in the world I wanted to see was Claude Friedrich at my doorstep.

You'd think he has the hots for me, I thought sardonically.

I parked the car in the carport and walked around to the front door instead of entering by the kitchen door, as I usually did.

"What do you want?" I asked curtly.

He raised his eyebrows. "Not very polite today, are we?"

"I've had a long day. I don't want to talk about the past. I want my supper."

"Then ask me in while you fix it." He said this quite gently.

I couldn't think of what to do, I was so surprised. I wanted to be alone, but I would sound peevish if I told him to go away—and what if he didn't?

Without answering, I unlocked the door and walked in. After a minute, he walked in behind me.

"Are you hungry or thirsty?" I said, fury just underneath the words.

"I've had my supper, but I'd appreciate a glass of tea if you have some," Friedrich rumbled.

Alone in the kitchen for a moment, I put my arms on the counter and rested my head on them. I heard the big man's footsteps sauntering through my spotless house, pausing in the doorway of my exercise room. I straightened and saw that Friedrich was in the kitchen, watching me. There was both sympathy and wariness in his face. I got a glass out of the cabinet and poured him some tea, plonking in some ice, too. I handed it to him wordlessly.

"I'm not here to talk about your past. I've had to check up on everyone connected to Pardon, as you can understand. Your name rang a bell. . . . I remembered it, from the newspapers. But what I'm here to talk about today . . . a client of yours was in to see me," Friedrich said. "He says you can verify his story."

I raised my eyebrows.

"Tom O'Hagen says he came in from playing golf on his day off, Monday, at about three o'clock."

He waited for my reaction, but I had none to give.

"He says that he then went over to Albee's apartment to pay his rent, found the apartment door ajar, looked inside, and saw that the area rug was rumpled up, the couch pushed crooked, and no one answered his call. He left his rent check on the desk right inside the door and left."

"So you're thinking Pardon may already have been dead at three o'clock."

"If Tom's telling the truth. You're his corroborating witness."

"How so?"

"He says he saw you going into the Yorks' apartment as he came down the stairs."

I thought back, trying hard to remember a perfectly ordinary day. I hadn't known until I was coming home from my night walk that it would be a day I needed to remember in detail.

I closed my eyes, attempting to replay that little stretch of time on Monday afternoon. I'd had the bag in my hand with the supplies the Yorks had wanted me to put in their apartment, anticipating their return. No, two bags. I'd had to put them down to fish out the right key—poor planning on my part. I remembered being peeved at my lack of foresight.

"I didn't hear anyone walking across the hall, but I did hear someone coming down the stairs, and it may have been Tom," I said slowly. "I was having trouble getting the right key separated from the bunch on my key chain. I went in the Yorks' place, put down the bags . . . put some things in the refrigerator. I left the other things out on the kitchen counter. I didn't need to water the asparagus plant because it was still very wet, and the shades in the bedroom were already open—I usually open them for the Yorks—so I left." I replayed locking the door, turning to leave. . . .

"I did see him! He was walking away from Pardon's apartment to go to his own and he was hurrying!" I exclaimed, pleased with myself. Tom O'Hagen isn't my favorite person, but I was glad I was able to verify his story, at least to some extent. If it had been Tom I'd heard coming down the stairs, and then I'd seen him again leaving Pardon's in the two or three minutes I'd spent in the Yorks' apartment, surely he wouldn't have had time to kill Pardon. But why would Tom have been upstairs? He has a ground-floor apartment. Deedra? Nope. She'd been at work.

"I hear you know Marshall Sedaka," Friedrich said abruptly. The comment was so unexpected that I actually looked at him directly.

"Yes."

"He was down to the station this morning, talking to Dolph Stafford. Dolph tells me he inherits that business now that Pardon Albee's dead. Pardon had a lot of irons in a lot of fires."

I raised both hands, palms up. What of it?

"No one here knows much about Marshall," Friedrich commented. "He just blew into town and married Thea Armstrong. No one could figure out why some man hadn't snatched Thea up years ago, her being so pretty and smart. Marshall got lucky, I figure. Now I hear he's moved out of the house, got himself a little rental place on Farraday."

I hadn't known where Marshall was living. Farraday was about three blocks away. I reached in the refrigerator, got out a container of soup I'd made over the weekend, and put it in the microwave.

It was a long two minutes until the timer beeped. I propped myself against the counter and waited for the police chief to go on.

"Pardon Albee was killed by one hard blow to the neck," Friedrich observed. "He was struck first on the mouth, and then got a crushing blow to the throat."

I thought of how strong Marshall is.

"So you're thinking," I said as I ladled soup into a bowl, "that Marshall dumped Thea for me and killed Pardon Albee so he'd own his business, now that he doesn't have Thea's twelve-thousand-dollar-a-year salary from SCC?"

Friedrich flushed. "I didn't say that."

"That's the only point I can grasp from all this. Could you tell me any other implication I might have missed?" I stared at him for a long moment, my eyebrows raised in query. "Right. Now, here's something real. Investigate *this.*" I held out the handkerchief, plain white, with a design of white stripes of different widths running around the border. Inside the handkerchief were the bumpy shapes of the gun and the handcuffs.

"You want to tell me about this?" Friedrich said.

Briefly and, I hope, unemotionally, I described what had happened at the Drinkwaters' that morning.

"You didn't call us? Someone was in the house with you and you didn't call us? Even if you were all right, what if they took something of Mel and Helen's?"

"I'm sure nothing was taken. I know everything in that house, and nothing was out of order. Nothing was rummaged through, or moved out of place, no drawers left open."

"You're assuming that these items were left by someone who knows about what happened to you in Memphis."

"Isn't that a logical assumption? I know you've found out. Have you told anyone?"

"No. It wasn't my business to do that. I did call the Memphis Police Department a couple of days ago. Like I said, I remembered where I'd heard your name—after I thought about it awhile. I've got to say, I'm kind of surprised you didn't change it."

"It's my name. Why would I change it?"

"Just to avoid anyone recognizing it, wanting to talk about what happened."

"For a while, I thought about it," I admitted. "But they'd already taken enough away from me. I wanted to keep at least my name. And then . . . it would have been like saying I had done something wrong." And I glared at Friedrich in a way that told him clearly he was not to comment. He sipped his tea thoughtfully.

I wondered if Pardon had known the truth about my past. He'd never even hinted as much to me, but he had been a man who liked to know things, liked to own a little piece of the people around him. If Pardon had known, surely he would have hinted around to me. He wouldn't have been able to resist it.

"So, did the Memphis police send you a report of some kind, something on paper?" I asked.

"Yes," he admitted. "They faxed me your file." He put his hand to his pocket, asked me if he could smoke his pipe.

"No," I said. "Where'd you leave the fax?"

"You think someone at my office has spread this around? You yourself haven't told anyone in this town about what happened to you?"

I lied. "I haven't told anyone. And whoever left these on the steps at the Drinkwaters' house knows I got raped, and knows the circumstances. So the knowledge had to come from your office, as far as I can tell."

Claude Friedrich's face darkened. He looked bigger, tougher, mean. "Lily, maybe someone has known since you moved here. Maybe they've just had the good taste not to mention it to you."

"Then they lost their good taste with a bang," I said. "You need to go. I have to work out."

He took the handkerchief, handcuffs, and gun with him when he left. I was glad not to have them in my house anymore.

Normally, I don't work out on Thursday nights, especially when I've already gone to Body Time in the morning. But the day had been one long accumulation of fear and anger, interrupted by the boredom of everyday work. I needed to do something to relax my shoulders, and the punching bag didn't appeal to me. I wanted weights.

I pulled on a pink spandex shorts and bra set, covered it with a flowered T-shirt, grabbed my workout bag, and drove to Body Time. Marshall doesn't work on Thursday nights, so I wouldn't have the emotional strain of seeing him while he was still trying to digest what I'd told him.

Derrick, the black college student who picks up the slack for Marshall in the evenings, waved a casual hand as I came in. The desk is to the left of the front door, and I stopped there to sign in before going over to the weight benches, unzipping my gym bag as I walked. There were only a couple of other people there, both serious bodybuilders, and they were doing leg work on the quad and calf machines and the leg press. I knew them only by sight, and after returning my nod, they ignored me.

The rest of the building was dark—no light in Marshall's office, the doors closed on the aerobics/karate room.

I stretched and did some light weights to warm up, then pulled on my weight-lifting gloves, padded across the palm and with the fingers cut off at the knuckle. I pulled the Velcro straps tight.

"Need me to spot?" Derrick called after I'd done three sets. I nodded. I'd done twenties, thirties, and forties, so I got the fifty-pound dumbbells from the rack and sat on one of the benches, lying down carefully with a dumbbell in each hand. When I felt Derrick's presence at my head, I checked my position. The dumbbells were parallel with the floor and I was holding them down at shoulder level. Then I lifted them up and in until they met over me.

"All *right,* Lily!" Derrick said. I brought the dumbbells down, then back up, fighting to maintain my control. Sweat popped out on my face. I was happy.

By the sixth repetition, the lift had begun to be a struggle. Derrick gripped my wrists, helping me just enough to enable me to complete the move. "Come on, Lily, you can do it," he murmured. "Push, now." And my arms rose yet another time.

I put the fifties on the rack and got the fifty-fives. With a great deal of effort, I lay down on the bench and struggled to lift them; the conventional wisdom at the gym is that the first time is the hardest, but in my experience, if the first time is really difficult, it's likely all the succeeding lifts will be tough, too. Derrick held my wrists as my arms ascended, loosened his grip as my arms came down. I lifted the fifty-fives six times, my lips pulled back from my teeth in a snarl of concentrated effort.

"One more," I gasped, feeling that treacherous exhaustion creeping through my arms. I was so focused on making my lift that until the dumbbells were triumphantly in the air, I didn't realize that the fingers helping me were ivory, not black.

I held the lift until my arms collapsed abruptly. "Going down!" I said urgently. Marshall moved back from the bench, and down came the weights, though I managed to stop short of dropping them from a height. I made a controlled drop, letting my bent arms hang down either side of the bench and releasing the dumbbells so they hit the rubber mat without rolling.

I sat up and swung around astride the bench, so pleased with my set that I overcame the anxiety of seeing Marshall for the first time after my true confessions session. Marshall was wearing what I thought of as his working clothes, a tank top and exotically patterned muscle pants from the line of exercise clothes clients could order through the gym.

"What happened to Derrick?" I asked, reaching for my gym bag to extract my pink sweat towel.

"I've been cruising all over town looking for you."

"What's wrong?"

"Have you been here all evening?"

"No. I got here . . . oh, thirty or forty minutes ago."

"Where were you before that?"

"At my house," I said, an edge coming into my voice. If anyone had been asking but Marshall, I would have refused to answer. The big room was very quiet. For the first time, I noticed that we were alone.

"Where's Derrick?" I asked again.

"I sent him home after your fifty set. Was anyone at your house?"

I stared at him while I patted my chest and face dry.

"What's your point?" I asked.

"Lily, about an hour and a half ago, someone came in Thea's back door while she was in the living room and left a dead rat on the kitchen table."

"Yuk," I said in disgust. "Who on earth would do something like that?" Suddenly, the dime dropped. "You think—" I was so outraged, I was sputtering for words, and my hands tightened into fists.

Marshall sat astride the other end of the bench; he reached over to put a finger to my lips. "No," he said urgently. "Never, I never thought so."

"Then why the questions?"

"Thea . . . she has this . . ."

I'd never heard Marshall flounder before. He was acutely embarrassed.

"Thea thinks I did it?"

Marshall looked at the blinds drawn over the big front window, closed for the night. "She thinks it might be you," he admitted.

"Why?" I was bewildered. "Why on earth would I do something like that?"

A flush spread across Marshall's cheeks.

"Thea has this idea that we're separated because of you."

"But Marshall . . . that's just crazy."

"Sometimes Thea is—crazy, I mean."

"Why would she think that?"

Marshall didn't answer.

"You can go back and tell Thea—or I will be more than glad to do it myself—that I had an unwelcome visit from the chief of police, at my home, until right before I left to come here. So I have what you might call a golden alibi."

Marshall drew a breath of sheer relief. "Thank God. Now maybe she'll leave me alone."

"So explain. Why would she think you two separated because of me?"

"Maybe I mentioned your name once too often when I was talking about karate class, or people who work out here."

Marshall's eyes met mine. I swallowed. I was suddenly, acutely, aware that we were alone. I could never remember being alone with Marshall before, truly alone in an empty building. He reached out and flicked the light switch, leaving us only in the light that came through the blinds from the street. It fell in stripes across his face and body.

We were still sitting astride the bench, facing each other. Slowly, giving me plenty of time to get used to the idea, he leaned forward until his mouth touched mine. I tensed, expecting the flood of panic that had marked my attempts to have a close relationship with a man during the past few years.

The panic didn't come.

My mouth moved against Marshall's, welcoming. He slid closer, his legs going under mine until I lifted mine to wrap around him, my feet resting on the bench behind him. My arms went around his back and his hands were behind my back, pressing me to him.

Maybe it was the unexpectedness of it, maybe it was the unthreatening setting, or maybe it was because I had known Marshall as a friend first, but suddenly what had been so difficult became easy and urgent.

Marshall's hand lifted my T-shirt over my head. He had already seen the scars: I didn't have that moment to fear. I pulled off his tank top, my hands shaking. His tongue moved in my mouth. My hands ran over his torso for the first time. He pulled up my athletic bra and my breasts popped out; his tongue found a new target. I made an anguished little sound as a part of me I'd thought was atrophied came surging back to life. My hands conveyed my urgency, and after a moment,

I stood, still straddling the bench, to work down my spandex shorts. He kissed my stomach as I stood before him, and then his mouth slid lower. In seconds, I rested one knee on the bench and turned to take my shorts off, and I heard cloth rustling in the darkness. Then bars of light fell across Marshall's heavily muscled bare body. In a few moments, Marshall was kneeling at the end of the bench while I lay back on it, filled with him, and the words he was whispering made me very happy, and everything worked beautifully.

Seven

I woke up cheerful, a condition so rare, I didn't even recognize it for a few minutes. I stretched in the bed, feeling a little sore in a most unusual way for me. Since I had had such a good workout the day before (and I smirked to myself when I thought that), I decided to do some push-ups at home rather than trek in to Body Time. I turned on the coffeepot and went into the room with the punching bag, then hit the floor and did fifty quick ones. I showered quickly and pulled on some loose-cut jeans and a T-shirt, my ordinary working clothes.

I have never figured out how other women think they are going to fight—*or* clean house—in skintight jeans.

After retrieving my paper, I sat down for some cereal and coffee. I was conscious all the time of being extraordinarily relaxed and pleased, a mood so unusual, I hardly knew how to handle it.

I caught myself beaming out the kitchen window at the lovely morning. It's truly amazing what a good screw can do for your outlook, I thought. And it wasn't just the wonderful physical sensation; it was the successful completion of the sex act without a panic attack or a wave of revulsion for my partner.

I found myself wondering if Marshall would call me that day. What would happen at class tonight? I crushed those thoughts ruthlessly. It had been what it was, good sex, nothing more. But boy, it sure was nice to remember.

I glanced at my watch, then reluctantly gathered up my portable caddy of cleaning materials and rags to set out for the first job of the day, Deedra Dean's apartment.

Deedra is supposed to be at work by eight, but today she was still getting ready when I knocked on the door before using her key. This wasn't the first time Deedra'd been late.

She had hot curlers in her hair and a black lace slip on her body. Marcus Jefferson was coming out of his door as Deedra opened hers, and Deedra made sure he got a good look at the slip. I stepped in and turned to shut the door, catching a good look at Marcus's face as I did so. He looked a little . . . disgusted—but excited.

I shook my head. Deedra stuck her tongue out at me as she flounced back to her bathroom to finish her face. I had to make a great effort not to slap her cheek in the hope of knocking some sense into her head; there must be some intelligence rattling around in there, since Deedra is able to hold down a job where she actually has to perform work.

"Lily!" she called from the bathroom as I stared grimly around the chaos of the apartment. "Are you a racist?"

"No, Deedra, I don't believe I am," I called back, thinking pleasurably of Marshall's ivory body. "But you're just playing—you're not serious about Marcus. And sleeping with a black man is still such a delicate thing that you really have to be serious about him to take the crap you're going to be handed."

"He's not serious, either," Deedra said, peeking out for a minute, one cheek pink and the other its natural white.

"Well, let's do something totally meaningless," I muttered, and began to pile up all the magazines and letters and bills scattered over the coffee table. I paused in midact. Was I the pot calling the kettle black? No, I decided with some relief, what Marshall and I did had some meaning. I'm not sure what yet. But it meant something.

I went about my business as though Deedra wasn't there, and I certainly wished she wasn't. Deedra hummed, sang, and chattered her way through the rest of her toilette, getting on my nerves to an incredible degree.

"What do you think will happen to us now that Pardon's dead?" Deedra asked as she buttoned up her red-and-black-striped dress. She slid her feet into matching pumps simultaneously.

"You're the third person to ask me what the fate of the apartment building will be," I said testily. "How should I know?"

"Why, Lily, we just figure you know it all," Deedra said matter-of-factly. "And you never tell; that's the nice thing about you."

I sighed.

"Now, that Pardon, what a son of a bitch," Deedra said in the same tone. "He sure was a pain to me. Always hovering, always asking me how my mama was, as if I needed reminding she's paying my rent for me. Always saying how nice it was I was dating so-and-so, if it was anybody white and professional, lawyer or doctor or bank president. Trying to scare me into living right."

I would have tried that, too, if I'd thought it would work,

I admitted to myself. Deedra was able to be flippant about Pardon Albee now that he was dead, but she'd been deathly afraid at the very idea of his searching her apartment the last time I'd talked to her.

The final button secured, Deedra went back to the bathroom mirror to add the finishing touches to her elaborately tousled blond hair.

She began in her nasal voice: "When I went to pay my rent Monday afternoon"—I jerked to attention—"I was going to have to plead with that old fart to keep his mouth shut about Marcus. He was asleep on the couch, though."

"What time was that?" I called, trying to sound casual.

"Ahm . . . four-thirtyish," Deedra said abstractedly. "I left work for a few minutes. I forgot to take him a check at lunchtime, and you know how he was about being paid by five." I walked down the hall so I could see her reflection in the mirror. Deedra was redefining an eyebrow.

"Did the apartment look okay?"

"Why, did you clean his, too?" Deedra said curiously, throwing down the eyebrow pencil. She began moving quickly to gather things up now that her face and hair were perfected. "Actually, the couch with its back to the door was pushed out of place. You know, it was on rollers. One end of it was touching the coffee table, and the throw rug in front of it was all runkled up."

"You stepped in and had a good look, huh?"

Deedra stopped dead in the act of reaching for her purse on the table by the door. "Hey, wait a minute," she said. "Hey, Lily, I just went inside the room when he didn't answer my knock. I thought maybe he was in the back of his apartment, since the door was unlocked. You know he was always home on rent day, and I thought it would be a good day to talk to him. I should have known better. It had already been a shitty day—my car wouldn't start, my boss shouted at me, and then on my way back to work I almost hit the camper. But anyway, I thought I heard a sound in the apartment, so I opened the door, and there he was, out like a light. So I left my check on the desk, since I saw some there already, and I tried to talk loud to wake him up a couple more times, but then I left."

"He wasn't asleep," I said. "He was dead."

Deedra's mouth fell open, obscuring her minimal chin entirely.

"Oh no," she whispered. "I never thought . . . I just assumed he was asleep. Are you sure?"

"Pretty sure." Though how to reconcile that with Tom O'Hagen's story—the rumpled rug, the couch sitting askew, but no body, an hour or more earlier—I couldn't fathom.

"You have to tell the police this," I said as Deedra continued to stand there in a stupor.

"Oh, I already did," Deedra said absently. "But they didn't tell me—Are you sure?"

"Pretty sure."

"So that's why he didn't hear me. And I was talking real loud."

"And did you tell them why you wanted to talk to Pardon?"

A glance at her tiny gold watch lit a fire under Deedra.

"Hell no! I just said I went down there to pay the rent." Deedra grabbed her keys, then glanced at herself once more in the big mirror over the couch. "And don't you tell, either, Lily Bard! They don't need to know anything about my personal life."

I had a lot to ponder after Deedra was out the door.

Pardon Albee's body had been on the couch of his apartment at 4:30, give or take fifteen minutes. It hadn't been there at three. But at three, when Tom saw it, the room was disarranged, the door left ajar, as though a struggle had taken place.

Where had the body been in the hours before I had watched it being trundled across the street into the arboretum?

I gathered up my cleaning things when Deedra's apartment looked habitable again, then locked the door behind me carefully. I didn't want to hear any more accusations like Deedra's last week. I went down the stairs slowly to the O'Hagen's. Cleaning their apartment would use up the rest of my Friday morning.

Jenny answered my knock, so I knew she'd had the two o'clock to ten o'clock shift at Bippy's the night before. After closing, the O'Hagen on night duty usually got home by eleven or twelve and slept in the next morning, while the other one had to get up at five o'clock to make the six o'clock opening. Shakespeare is a town that rises early and beds early.

Jenny has red hair and freckles, a flat chest, and wide hips, and she dresses well to camouflage those features. But today in her flowered bathrobe, she was not aiming to impress me. Jenny likes to regard me as part of the furniture, anyway. After saying hi indifferently, Jenny plopped back in her recliner and lit a cigarette, her eyes returning to a talk show I had never thought of watching.

Jenny was the only person I'd seen in the past five days who was acting completely normal.

The O'Hagens do their own laundry, but Jenny and Tom hate cleaning their kitchen, not too surprising when you consider they manage a restaurant. So I almost always have plenty to load in the dishwasher, sometimes what I estimate to be a whole week's worth, and the garbage is always full of micro-wave meal trays and heat-and-eat cans. It also isn't too sur-prising, I figure, that they don't want to cook when they are home.

Jenny ignored me utterly as I moved around the apartment, to the point of not reacting at all when I took everything off the TV tray table set up next to the recliner and dusted the tray, putting its contents back in pleasing order after-ward. I hate Jenny's cigarette smoke; she is the only client I have who smokes, I realized with a little surprise.

The phone rang after I'd had been working an hour. I heard Jenny pick it up and turn down the volume on the television set. Without trying, I heard Jenny murmur into the receiver for a few minutes, then thunk it back in its cradle.

I had worked my way back to the master bedroom, where I changed the sheets in a flash and snapped the bedspread back into order. I dumped the ashtray on Jenny's side of the bed (red hair on that pillow) and was walking around the bed to empty Tom's ashtray when Jenny appeared in the doorway.

"Thanks for backing up Tom," she said abruptly.

I glanced up, trying to read the round freckled face. All I could see was reluctance. Jenny didn't like feeling beholden.

"Just told the truth," I said, dumping the butts into the gar-bage bag and wiping out the ashtray. I replaced it with a little clunk on the bedside table. I spied a pencil on the floor, stooped to pick it up, and dropped it in the drawer of the bedside table.

"I know Tom's story sounded a little funny," Jenny said ten-tatively, as though she was waiting for my reaction.

"Not to me," I said crisply. I scanned the bedroom, couldn't spot anything I'd missed, and started out the door to the second bedroom, which the O'Hagens had fitted up as an office. Jenny stepped back to let me pass.

I'd tucked the corner of the dust cloth into my belt as I finished the bedroom. Now I whipped it out and began dusting the office. To my surprise, Jenny followed me. I glanced at my watch and kept on working. I was due at the Winthrops' by one, and I wanted to have something for lunch before I got there.

The glance wasn't lost on Jenny. "Keep right on working," she said invitingly, as though I wasn't already. "I just wanted you to know we appreciate your remembering correctly. Tom was relieved he didn't have to answer any more questions."

One had occurred to me during the morning. In the normal course of things, it wouldn't have crossed my mind to ask Jenny, but I was fed up with Jenny alternately ignoring me and following me around.

"So, did the police ask him what he was doing coming down the stairs from the other apartments, when he lives on the ground level?" I asked. I had my back to Jenny, but I heard a sharp intake of breath that signaled shock.

"Yes, Claude did, just now," Jenny said "He wanted to ask Tom about that, since Tom hadn't mentioned that earlier."

I could see why Claude Friedrich would think of asking, since his own apartment was on the second floor, opposite Norvel Whitbread's.

"And what did Tom say?"

"None of your business," flashed Jenny.

Now, this was the familiar Jenny O'Hagen.

"Guess not," I said. I ran the dust cloth over the metal parts of the rolling chair behind the desk.

"Well . . ." Jenny trailed off, then turned and marched into her bedroom, closing the door behind her firmly.

She emerged just as I finished cleaning—which I did not exactly consider a coincidence—clad in a bright green camp shirt and gray slacks.

"It looks great, Lily," Jenny said without looking around. So she'd reverted to the new Jenny. I preferred the familiar rude Jenny; at least then I knew where I stood.

"Um-hm. You want to write me a check now, or mail it to me?"

"Here's the money in cash."

"Okay." I wrote a receipt, tucked the money in my pocket, and turned to leave.

I could feel Jenny moving up behind me, and I spun quickly, to discover she was much closer.

"It's okay!" Jenny said hastily, backing up. "I just wanted to tell you that Tom wasn't doing anything wrong on the second floor, okay? He was up there, but it was okay." To my amazement, Jenny looked red around the eyes and nose, as though she was about to cry.

I hoped that Jenny wouldn't actually weep; I would not pat Jenny O'Hagen on the back.

Evidently, Jenny felt the same way. "See you next week," she said in a clogged voice.

I shrugged, picked up my caddy of cleaning materials, and left. "Good-bye," I said over my shoulder, to prove I was not uncivil.

I'd closed the door briskly behind me as if I intended to leave the building at my usual clip. But I stopped and looked up and down the hall. There was no one in sight; I could hear no movement in the building. It was about noon on a Friday, and aside from the Yorks and Mrs. Hofstettler, everyone should be at work.

It had occurred to me that the closet under the stairs (Where Pardon kept odds and ends like extra lightbulbs and the heavy-duty vacuum for the halls) would have been an excellent temporary resting place for Pardon's wandering corpse.

And it just so happened I had a key.

Pardon himself had given it to me three years before, when he'd taken the only vacation I could remember. He'd gone to Cancún with a bus tour made up mostly of other Shakespeareans. While he'd been gone, I'd had the job of cleaning the halls and the glass panels in the back door, making sure the parking lot was clear of garbage, and channeling all the residents' complaints to the proper repairman. Pardon had given me the key then, and he had never asked for its return, perhaps anticipating more package tours in his future.

But all his fussing about his health had proved to have some basis, finally, when a specialist in Little Rock had told Pardon his heart actually had some small problem. Pardon had sworn off tours forever, for fear he'd have some kind of crisis in a foreign place, and he never tired of showing people his Cancún photos and telling them of his near brush with death.

I'd marked all the keys entrusted to me with my own code. If they were stolen, I didn't want the thief to be able to get into my clients' homes and offices. The code I used was not sophisticated: I just went down to the next letter of the alphabet, so the key to the closet of Shakespeare Garden Apartments had a little strip of masking tape on it with the initials THB in heavy black ink.

I tossed my key ring up and caught it with my right hand while I debated whether to look or not.

Yes, I decided.

The disappearance and reappearance of Pardon's body, and its ultimate disposal in the park via my cart, had opened a vein of curiosity and anger in me. For one thing, it revealed unexpected depths in one of the people I saw often—for I didn't think it possible that the killer could be someone other than an apartment resident.

I didn't know I'd reached that conclusion until I had the key in the lock and was turning it.

I looked inside the large closet. It opens facing the hallway, and since it conforms to the rise of the staircase, it is much higher at the left end than the right. I reached up for the long string that hangs down from the bare bulb overhead. Just as my hand touched it, a voice spoke behind me.

"What you looking for, Miss Lily?"

I gasped involuntarily, but in a second, I recognized the voice. I turned around to face Claude Friedrich.

"Anything I can help you with?" he continued as I looked up, trying to read the broad face.

"God Almighty, where *were* you?" I asked ferociously, angry at myself that I hadn't heard him, angry at him for the fear he'd made me feel.

"In Pardon's apartment."

"Just skulking?"

I was not going to be able to provoke him into anger so he'd forget to ask me again, I saw.

"Examining the scene of the crime," he said genially. "And wondering, as I suspect you are, how come one person sees a body on the couch at four-thirty after someone else saw an empty couch at three o'clock, though at three o'clock the apartment looked like someone'd had a fight."

"Pardon could've survived for a while," I said, surprising myself by simply telling the policeman what was on my mind.

He looked equally surprised, and rather pleased.

"Yes, indeed, if it'd been another kind of wound." Friedrich nodded his head of thick graying hair slowly. "But with that blow to the neck, he would have suffocated pretty quick."

And he looked down at my hands, empty now, since I'd put down the cleaning caddy when I opened the door. My hands looked thin and bony and strong.

"I could have killed him," I said, "but I didn't. I had no reason to."

"What if Pardon had said he was going to spread the story of your bad time all over town?"

"He didn't know." I'd come to that conclusion early this morning. "You know what Pardon was like. He loved knowing all about everyone, and he'd bust a gut to tell whoever it was that he'd found out something about them. He'd have loved to *sympathize* with me about what happened. No one knew until you called Memphis and left that report lying around." That was something else I'd have to do on my own—find out who in the police department had been talking, and to whom. I thought it quite likely that whoever had planted the cuffs and gun on the Drinkwaters' stairs had learned the significance of those items from a loose-mouthed police department employee.

"Probably you're right on that," Friedrich admitted, giving me a pleasant surprise in return for the one I'd given him, "and I'm looking into it. So you're checking out the closet to see if that's where he was stowed?"

I blinked at the change of subject. Friedrich was touchy about my reference to the poor security at the police department, as well he might be.

"Yes." I explained how I came to have the key.

"Well, let's look," Friedrich suggested, with a geniality I distrusted.

"You've already looked," I said.

"Actually, no. Pardon's key ring hasn't turned up. We didn't want to break down the door. A locksmith was coming this morning to open it up, but now you've saved the city of Shakespeare a little money. I never thought of asking you if you had a key."

It didn't seem a good time to tell him that I had keys to the front and back doors of the building, too.

"Why didn't you ask Norvel Whitbread?" I asked. "He was supposed to be working for Pardon one morning a week."

"He said he didn't have a key. And it seemed likely to me that Pardon wouldn't trust him enough to give him one, that Pardon would unlock the closet for him if Norvel needed to get in."

I tucked the puzzle of Pardon's missing key ring in with all the other elements involved in the strange death of the landlord.

Friedrich stepped past me, reached up to pull the string, and scanned the closet when the light flooded into every corner. Pardon, whatever his faults, had not been stingy with wattage.

"Does it look like it always does, as far as you can tell?" Friedrich asked after we'd both taken a good look.

"Yes," I said, a little disappointed. The shelves to the rear and left side of the closet were neatly lined with necessities—

garbage bags, lightbulbs, cleaning materials—and odds and ends that Pardon had thought might be useful someday— mousetraps, vases, a doorknob, the big doorstop Pardon used to hold the front door when he got the hall carpet cleaned and it was still damp. The big vacuum cleaner took up the right side of the closet. It was ancient, huge, and parked neatly, with its cord wrapped in a precise coil. That proved Norvel hadn't vacuumed last; Norvel would never wind a cord that pretty, I thought admiringly.

But Norvel was supposed to be doing the janitorial work.

Friedrich was looking over the shelves carefully and thought-fully, apparently doing an item-by-item inventory.

I reached over to touch his sleeve, then thought the better of it. "Excuse me," I said.

"Yes'm?" Friedrich said abstractedly.

"Look at the cord on the vacuum." I waited till he'd taken a good look. "Someone other than Norvel Whitbread put that vacuum in here, and Norvel was supposed to do it." I explained why I thought so.

Friedrich looked mildly amused. "You got any idea who might have put the vacuum in here, based on the way the cord is coiled?" he asked, and I realized he was gently pulling my leg.

Ho-ho. "Yes, I have. I've seen the way Pardon put things away. That's the way Pardon did it. Every Monday morning, before he went to the church, Norvel was supposed to vacuum and clean the glass in the doors, sweep the front walkway, and pick up trash in the parking area in the back. It doesn't seem he did that on Monday."

"That's a lot to infer from a vacuum cleaner."

It was an effort to shrug indifferently.

I took the key to the closet off my ring and handed it to Friedrich. Before he could say anything, I hoisted my caddy and strode out the front door, evicting Friedrich from my thoughts. I cast around in my mind for any reason I needed to go in my house; all of a sudden, I wasn't hungry anymore. Maybe I should jump right in the car to go to the Winthrops' house.

But there was yet another bump in my path—a car parked, blocking mine, in my driveway, and someone standing in my carport, leaning against my Skylark. My heart lurched when I recognized Marshall. I stood there awkwardly, not knowing what to do or say, feeling my cheeks get hot.

He took the caddy from me and put it on the ground. He drew me farther up under the carport and put his arms around me. After a moment, my arms went around his neck.

"I couldn't call you," he said in my ear. "I didn't know what to say over the telephone. I don't know what to say now."

If he didn't, I sure wasn't going to venture anything. I was managing to enjoy being held, but I didn't like being in the carport; I didn't want to be seen. But the intoxication of Marshall's nearness, his remembered smell and touch, began to chip away at my anxiety. I felt a little dizzy. His tongue touched my lips.

"Marshall, I have to work," I managed to say.

He held me a little away, looked at me sharply.

"Lily, are you putting me off because you don't want to be with me? Are you sorry about last night?"

"No." I shook my head to reinforce it. "No."

"Are you having trouble, remembering what happened to you?"

"No . . ." I hesitated. "But you know, having had sex

once successfully doesn't mean I'm never going to live in the shadow of the rape again. The rest of my life, I'll have to deal with it."

I am not a trouble-free woman. I am not always user-friendly. He had to have that brought to his attention, if he was trying to ignore it.

"But really, and I regret this, I'm late to my next cleaning job," I finished prosaically.

"Lily," he said again, as if he enjoyed saying it. I'd been looking down at the spot where our chests were touching. Now I met his eyes. His mouth came toward mine, and I could feel he was ready.

"We can't now," I whispered apologetically.

"Tonight, after class?"

"Okay."

"Don't eat first; we'll fix something at my place."

I never ate before calisthenics, anyway. I nodded, and smiled at him. A red car going by in the street alerted me to the passage of time. I looked at my watch over his shoulder, wishing I could afford to call the Winthrops and tell them I was sick. But Marshall was an anomaly, and my work was the norm.

I was beginning to hope that with Marshall I could be exactly who I felt like being. The Memphis Lily, the Lily with long brown hair, who puffed and panted after twenty minutes on the treadmill, would never have done what blond strong Lily did to Marshall next. My caress made him shiver all over.

"You don't know what it's been like," he said when he could speak. I realized that Marshall had a story to tell, too.

"If you're sure you don't have ten extra minutes now," he

went on breathlessly, "I guess I'll have to wait until tonight. We better not spar together in class!"

I found myself smiling at the thought of Marshall seething with desire while blocking my kicks, and seeing me smile made him laugh out loud.

"See you then," I said, with a sudden resurgence of shyness. I gently extricated myself from his arms and went to my car. As he passed me to go to his Toyota, I had a back view of broad shoulders and tight butt to admire.

It had been so long since my plans had extended beyond my latest batch of library books or a movie I'd rented that I hardly knew what to think of as I drove the familiar route to my next job. I would be sweaty after class. Could I shower at his house? Would he expect me to stay the night, or would I come home to sleep? Where would I park my car? It was nobody's business that I would be visiting Marshall's rental house. I liked my life private.

As I slid out of my car at the Winthrops' back door, I decided I was excited, and scared. But most of all, I felt unsettled, a feeling I was having trouble enjoying. I'm not used to having so many variables to contend with, I realized.

But I had to put all that away in the back of my mind and get to work. I let myself in, locked the door behind me, and looked around the kitchen. The cook, Earline Poffard, had been at work; the counter was spotless and there was a full garbage can under the sink. Earline comes in twice a week, and she cooks enough suppers for the Winthrops to eat until she comes again. I had never met Earline face-to-face, but I knew her from her work; Earline labels everything she prepares, all her garbage lands in the bag, and she scours all the dishes herself, drys them, and puts them away. I have only to clean the outside of the microwave and the door of the dishwasher from time to time, and mop, and the kitchen cleaning is done.

For the first time, it occurred to me that I would like to meet Earline. Perhaps Earline was equally curious about me.

The habits of years reasserted themselves, and I set to work. I didn't want to be late to class this night; I looked forward to seeing Marshall my lover, and I didn't want Marshall my sensei to be shooting me the disapproving look he'd given me last time.

I'd gotten the dusting done and was getting the mop out of the closet when I heard a key in the lock.

"Hey, Lily," called a casual male voice.

"Hi, Bobo," I replied, making a mental note to tell Beanie she needed a new mop.

"Hey, what about that old guy getting killed over by your place?" Bobo said, his voice getting closer.

I glanced over my shoulder. The boy—the six-foot-two boy—was leaning against the kitchen sink, looking spectacular in cutoffs and an Umbro shirt. His grin betrayed his age, but his body had grown up ahead of him. I answer the phone while I'm working at the Winthrops', and most of the calls in the summer are inevitably for Bobo. He has his own phone, of course, but he gives only particular friends that number, much to his mother's irritation.

"He died," I said.

"That's no answer, Lily! C'mon, you must know all about it."

"I'm sure you know as much about it as I do."

"Is it true someone called old Claude Friedrich while he was sacked out and told him where the body was?"

"Yes."

"See, now that's the kind of thing I want you to tell me."

"You already knew that, Bobo." My patience had almost evaporated.

"Well . . . give me the inside scoop. You gotta know something that wasn't in the paper, Lily."

"I doubt it." Bobo loved to talk, and I knew he'd follow me around the house if I gave him the slightest encouragement.

"How old are you, Bobo?" I asked.

"Oh, I'm a senior. I'm seventeen," he said. "That's why I'm outta class early today. You gonna miss me next year when I go off to college, Lily?"

"You know it, Bobo." I got the Mop & Glow from the cupboard, then turned the sink water to hot. "For one thing, I ought to charge your parents less money because I won't have your mess to clean up."

"Oh, by the way, Lily . . ."

When he didn't finish his sentence, I glanced over, to see Bobo was blushing a bright red.

As I raised my eyebrows to show I was waiting for him to finish his sentence, I squirted some cleaner on the floor. The water was running hot; I squeezed out the excess water and began to mop.

"When you were cleaning my room the other day, did you happen to find . . . something . . . ah, personal?"

"Like the condom?"

"Um. Right. Yeah." Bobo stared at something fascinating by his right foot.

"Um-hmm."

"What'd you do with it?"

"What do you mean? I threw it away. You think I was going to sleep with it under my pillow?"

"I mean . . . did you tell my mom? Or my dad?"

"Not my business," I said, noting that Howell Winthrop, Jr., came a decided second on the list of people Bobo feared.

"Thanks, Lily!" Bobo said enthusiastically. He met my eyes briefly, his shoulders relaxed: He was a man looking at blue skies.

"Just keep using them."

"What? Oh. Oh, yeah."

And Bobo, if possible, grew redder than before. He left with a great show of nonchalance, jingling his keys and whistling, obviously feeling he'd had an adult conversation about sex with an older woman. I was willing to bet he'd be more careful disposing of personal items in the future, as well he ought.

I found myself singing as I worked, something I hadn't done in years. I sing hymns when I'm by myself; I know so many, from the countless Sundays I'd spent sitting with my parents and Varena in church—always in the same pew, fifth from the front on the left. I found myself remembering the mints my mother always had in her purse, my father's pen and the notepad he produced for me to draw on when I got too restless.

But thinking of my childhood seldom brings me anything but pain. Back then, my parents hadn't cast their eyes down when they spoke to me. They'd been able to hold conversations without tiptoeing verbally around anything they thought might distress their ravaged daughter. I'd been able to hug them without bracing myself for the contact.

From long practice, I was able to block out this unproductive and well-traveled train of thought. I concentrated on the pleasure of singing. It's always an amazement to me that I have a pretty voice. I'd had lessons for a few years; I used to sing solo in church, and perform at weddings from time to time. Now I sang "Amazing Grace." I reached up to brush the hair out of my face when I was finished, and it was a shock to find it was short.

Eight

I'd almost forgotten my sedentary neighbor's participation in the Wednesday-night class. It sure hadn't looked like he was having a good time, so I was surprised to see Carlton warming up when I bowed in the doorway. He was trying to touch his toes. I could tell from the way his mouth twisted that movement was painful.

"The full soreness has set in, huh?" I said as I sat on the floor to pull off my shoes.

"Even my hair hurts," he said through clenched teeth as he strained downward. His fingers just managed to touch the tops of his feet.

"This is your worst day," I told him.

"Is that supposed to make me feel better?"

"I thought maybe it would help to know that tomorrow won't be so bad." I rolled my socks in a neat ball and stuck them in my right shoe. I stood, rotated my neck gently, then bent from my waist and put my hands flat on the floor. I gave a sigh of pleasure as my back stretched and the tension of the day flowed out.

"Show off," Carlton said bitterly.

I straightened and looked him over. Carlton was wearing shorts and a T-shirt. To the untrained eye, he would have looked pretty good, but I could see the lack of definition and development in his arms and thighs. Overweight, he wasn't; in shape, he wasn't.

Marshall came in and gave me a private smile before one of the other students approached him with a question. I followed him with my eyes for a moment and then considered Carlton, who was on the floor, his legs spraddled to either side, trying to touch his chest to the right leg, then the left. Carlton's thick black hair, normally gelled and swept behind his ears, was getting wild as he straightened and bent, straightened and bent. I pulled the top of my gi out of my gym bag and slid into it, then tended to the tying of the belt.

"So, Carlton. Remember the subduing hold we practiced last time?" I asked. Carlton scrambled to his feet.

"Ah . . . no. I had so much to learn that one night."

Marshall was laughing with a knot of the younger men in the class.

"Okay. Reach out to grab my gi with your right hand. . . . That's right. Now, grip hard." Apparently scared he'd pull me off balance, Carlton barely took hold of the loose material. "No, Carlton. You really have to hold on, or you'll think I was able to do this because you weren't exerting full strength."

Carlton, while increasing the force of his grip, looked distinctly anxious. "Oh, I wouldn't think that!" he protested.

"Now, remember? I reach up with my right hand, like so. . . . I sink my thumb into the pit between your thumb and forefinger, to hit the pressure point—I got it, I see—and then I twist your hand so that the outside of it, the side of your little finger, is pointed toward the ceiling. . . . Of course that rotates your whole arm, right?"

I could tell Carlton was remembering.

"Now I press your knuckles to my chest, being careful to keep your arm rotated. My fingers are wrapped around your hand, to keep the tension on. . . . My thumb's still applying pressure . . . and now I—"

"Nooooo," moaned Carlton, dropping to his knees as I applied counterpressure with my left hand on his upper arm and then bent over from the waist.

"Remember the distress signal Marshall showed you last time?" I asked.

Carlton shook his head, deeply involved with his pain.

"Slap your thigh with your free hand."

He lost no time slapping, and I let go instantly.

He looked up at me, his brown eyes wide in a pleading spaniel look that I suppose had been very effective on other women.

"That really hurt," he said after a significant pause.

"We don't apologize, Carlton," I said gently. "I taught you something. We all get hurt."

Carlton stood up, shook himself. He was having a little struggle with pride; his sensible side won.

"Well, here I am, learning," he said ruefully. "So I assume, to show you I learned it correctly, I get to do it to you?"

I reached out and grabbed his T-shirt.

I had to talk Carlton through the steps of hurting me enough for it to count. "Sorry, I don't have to go down. . . . Twist my hand a little more. . . . Now go slow. You really don't want to break my arm. Wait for a real fight for that. . . . Raphael, what is Carlton doing wrong?"

"He's not keeping you close enough," diagnosed Raphael.

"Okay, Carlton, you're backing off, which means I can get free, or I can at least kick you and make you let go. . . ." To demonstrate, I lashed out with my foot suddenly, but I pulled back in time just to tap Carlton's groin.

With a gasp, Carlton let go.

"We'll practice later," I said. "You might feel better doing this with Raphael or one of the other guys, because most men get so anxious about hurting a woman partner that they don't give it their best shot."

"That bother you?" he asked.

"It used to. Now I think that in the real world, it would work to my advantage, and since women don't have men's upper-body strength, I need all the edge I can get." I eyed Carlton with my own curiosity. "Why'd you really start coming?"

"I wanted to see what you were so gung ho about. Three nights a week, for years . . . never missing, always on time. I thought it must be something that was a lot of fun."

"It is," I said, surprised that it could be seen differently.

"The fun is not apparent yet," Carlton said. I hadn't known his voice could be so dry.

"Oh, it will be. You just have to learn a little, and it won't be so confusing." Marshall was about to begin class, so I went to my place in line. I wasn't convinced that Carlton found me of such overwhelming interest that he felt like following my schedule, especially after our little exchange at my house earlier in the week.

"Kiotske!" Marshall called, and the class came to attention.

At water-break time, after calisthenics, Marshall drifted over to me. I could tell he was aiming for me, I was aware every minute of what he was doing as he said a word to this student or that. I was excited by his nearness, but I had not the slightest idea what to say to him.

"Did you hear anything else about what happened to Thea?" I asked after we'd given each other a little nod of greeting.

"No. The police said fingerprinting the doors didn't bring up anything unusual, and none of her neighbors saw anything. That little house has a grown-up backyard, so that's not too surprising. At least the rat was probably just caught in a trap, not tortured or anything."

"Was she very shook-up?"

Marshall's expression was peculiar. "Thea's pretty emotional," he said.

I wondered if Thea had pleaded with him to come home for her protection, a thought I found distasteful. I didn't want to set foot in the situation between Marshall and Thea. But of course if you have sex with a man, I told myself wryly, you're part of the situation between him and his wife automatically.

As I practiced buntai with Janet Shook, the only other woman who consistently came to class, it occurred to me that the hideous practical joke played on me at the Drinkwaters' might be related to the equally hideous prank played on Thea. Was someone else so enamored of Marshall that she was doing horrible things to women she perceived as being involved with him?

As much as the thought made my skin crawl, it at least made some kind of sense out of an otherwise-bewildering incident.

"Lily!" Marshall called. Janet and I stopped our striking-and-blocking practice, and I bowed to Janet briefly before running over to Marshall. He was standing with Carlton, and he looked a little exasperated. "You're a good teacher, Lily. Carlton and I are not—we're not meshing gears on star drill, and I need to help Davis on his kata. Could you . . ."

"Sure," I said. Marshall patted my shoulder and moved on to Davis, a weedy twentyish man who sold insurance.

"Sorry you're stuck with me," Carlton said, though he didn't look particularly sorry.

"What part of this exercise are you having trouble with?"

"The whole thing."

I sighed, not too quietly.

"Okay, specifically, I'm having trouble remembering the sequence."

"All right. Get in shiko dachi. . . . No, turn your feet out. . . . Now squat some more."

Carlton moaned.

I dropped into position facing him. "Now, *you* face that way," I told him, pointing to my right, "and *I'll* face this way. . . . No, keep your hips in position; just turn the upper torso. . . ."

"Explain to me again why we're whacking our arm bones together," Carlton said pathetically.

"To make them tougher. So we don't feel as much pain when we fight."

"We go through it now so we don't feel it later?"

"Ah . . . right. Now, forearms down, up . . . switch sides! Forearms down, up, switch!"

"So," he puffed after a few more seconds, "what would you do right now if I leaned over and kissed you on the neck?"

"Well, you're standing in a position that leaves your genitals wide open. So I'd probably strike you seiken—that is, with a powerful jab, in the groin, and then when you doubled over, I'd get you with an elbow to the back of the neck, and when you were all the way on the floor, I'd kick you repeatedly."

"Better not do that, then."

"Better not."

"Just wanted to find out."

"There is something else I want from you."

"Name it."

"I want to know who's inheriting the apartments and all Pardon's other land holdings, if he has any."

Carlton grunted as I accidentally elbowed him. "A niece of Pardon's, the daughter of Pardon's dead sister. She called Pardon's lawyer yesterday, who called me, since she's going to be coming to town day after tomorrow to arrange for Pardon's burial. Ow, Lily! Not so hard! And go over his books with me. This gal lives in Austin, Texas. I'm sure you're gonna love her. She's a tae kwon do instructor. Pardon had mentioned her to me one time."

"Could that be why you're suddenly interested in coming here, rather than curiosity about my schedule?"

"Fifty-fifty, I'd say."

"I'd better warn you, goju is really different from tae kwan do. Philosophy, fighting technique, stances."

I shut up and accelerated the star drill until Carlton suddenly gave out. I'd been picking up the signals (shaking legs, increased sweating, a desperately determined set to his mouth) but had ignored them ruthlessly.

"Give me a break!" Carlton said, and I felt a little shame at driving him so hard.

"Don't scare him away, Lily," Marshall said behind me.

"No, sir." I tried to look repentant.

"Back in line," Marshall called to the paired students, and we scampered (or hobbled) back into place.

"Kiotske!" We came to attention. "Rai!" We bowed. "Class dismissed!"

"My favorite words," Carlton murmured to Janet, who laughed—too much for such a feeble joke, I thought.

Marshall came up to me and said very quietly, "I'll pick you up at your house," which answered all my questions.

I sat on the floor to pull on my shoes. After I tied them, it was an effort to get up smoothly, but it was also a point of pride. Carlton was sitting in one of the folding chairs that lined the room, his head cocked. He was looking at me as if he was examining a suspect hundred-dollar bill.

"Good night," I said briefly.

"Good night," he answered, and bent to tie his sneakers, a scowl on his handsome face.

I shrugged and went through the double doors, passing Marshall's office and waving to him. He was looking at employee time sheets. The main room was empty except for Stephanie Miller, one of Marshall's hired hands who teaches some of the aerobic classes. Stephanie was running the big industrial vacuum cleaner over the worn green carpet. I gave her a casual nod and passed through the front door and over to my Skylark, one of four cars left in the parking lot. There was something on the hood of my car.

I wouldn't let myself stop, but I slowed down to get a better look. It was a . . . doll?

Then I was standing a foot away and I dropped my gym bag. It was a doll, a Ken doll.

The eye had been defaced with red nail polish. It was fresh. I could smell it from where I stood. It had been used to create artistic drops of blood down the doll's face. Someone had made the doll look as if it had been shot in the left eye, the eye I had hit when I shot Nap.

I remembered exactly how it had looked, the sound the man had made, the way he'd hit the floor. He hadn't looked anything like a Ken doll. . . .

"What's wrong?" Carlton asked. "Car trouble?"

I was glad to be dragged back from the edge of the nightmare. I stood back so Carlton could see.

"Was this on your car?"

"Yes. I left the car locked, so someone put it on the hood."

I shivered at the malignancy of the "gift."

"What's up?" Marshall asked. He'd just locked the front doors of the gym. Across the parking lot, Stephanie got in her car and pulled out to go home.

I pointed to the doll. I couldn't bring myself to touch it.

"Oh, Lily, I'm sorry," he said after a moment.

"I get the feeling there's something about this I don't know?" Carlton asked.

I puffed out my cheeks with a gust of air. I was so tired. "I guess I ought to take this by the police station," I said.

"Lily, let it wait until tomorrow," Marshall said. "Go on home now. I'll see you in a little while."

"No. I want to get rid of it. I'll call you when I get home."

"Lily, do you want me to go to the police station with you?" Carlton asked.

I'd had almost forgotten Carlton was still there. I found myself feeling the unaccustomed emotions of warmth and gratitude toward my neighbor.

"That's very kind of you," I said stiffly, wishing I could

sound more gracious. "But I think I better go by myself. Thank you for offering."

"Okay. If you need me, call me." Carlton hobbled over to his Audi and went home, doubtless anticipating a hot bath and a welcoming bed.

I watched him go because I didn't want to turn to meet Marshall's eyes.

"I'm wondering," I said, still looking into the night, "whether you have a secret admirer—someone who could find out my history and leave these little gifts for me, someone who could kill a rat and leave it on Thea's table."

"So, it's scaring you off, and we should forget about us?" Marshall leaped to the thought. He was upset and angry.

Well, I'm not exactly happy, either, I fumed to myself.

"No, that's not what I'm saying."

"Are you saying you don't want to see me tonight?"

"I don't know. No, that's not what I'm saying. I've been looking forward to it as much as you have." I raised my hands, palms upward, in a gesture of frustration. "But this is bad, isn't it? To think someone's watching me? Sneaking around with things like this?" I waved my hand toward the doll. "Thinking about what to do to me next?"

"So you'll let that person make your life even more miserable?"

I swung around to face Marshall so suddenly that his shoulders tensed. I had so many thoughts, it was a struggle as to which one would be voiced first. "I think I gave that up a good many years ago," I said. I was stiff with fury, felt like hurting him. "And while I looked forward to screwing you tonight, missing it would not make me miserable."

"I wanted to sleep with you, too," Marshall said, equally

angry now. "But I also wanted just to be with you. Just talk to you. Have a normal conversation with you—if that's possible."

I struck, aiming for his diaphragm. Like a senseless person who didn't want teeth anymore, I told myself later. Quicker than I could block with my left arm, Marshall's hand shot out and gripped the wrist of my striking right arm when my knuckles were within an inch of his abdomen. His other hand had formed the knife, and was starting for my neck. For a long moment, we stared at each other, eyes wide and angry, before coming to our senses. His hand relaxed and he placed his fingers gently against my throat, feeling my pulse racing. My fist uncurled and fell to my side.

"Almost got you," I said, embarrassed to find my voice was shaking.

"Almost," he admitted. "But you would've been down first."

"Not so," I argued. "The diaphragm blow would've doubled you over and you would've missed my neck."

"But the blow would've landed somewhere," he argued back, "and the force would have knocked you backward. Admittedly, after you had already hit me . . ." His voice trailed off and we looked at each other sheepishly.

"Maybe," I said, "I'm not the only person who has trouble carrying on a 'normal' conversation?"

"You're right. This is probably pretty weird."

Very carefully, as though we were covered with thorns, we eased into each other's arms.

"Relax," whispered Marshall. "Your neck muscles are like wires."

I tentatively laid my head on his shoulder. I turned my mouth into his neck. "What I'm going to do," I said gently, "is take the doll to the police department, tell them where I found it, and go home. When I get there, I'll call you. You'll come get me. We'll eat at your place, and then we'll do good things together."

His hand massaged my neck. "I can't get you to reverse the order?"

"I'll see you soon," I promised, then slid from his arms and got in the car, stowing the grotesque doll on the seat beside me. I drove to the police department, which is housed in a former drugstore a couple of blocks from the center of town. There was only one police car in the parking lot, a dark blue city of Shakespeare car with a big number 3 on the side.

Tom David Meiklejohn was sitting inside, his feet propped up on a desk. He had an RC Cola in one hand and a cigarette in the other. Tom David, whom I know by sight, is good-looking in what I think of as a honky-tonk way. He has short, curly hair, bright, mean eyes flanking a sharp nose, and thin lips, and he dresses western on his days off. He'd been sleeping with Deedra around last Christmas, and during that month or two I'd seen him go in and out of the Garden Apartments regularly.

Tom David had been married at the time to a woman as hard-edged as he was, or so one travel agent had told another as I was cleaning their office. A few months later, I had seen the Meiklejohns' divorce notice in the local paper.

Now, Tom David, whom I'd observed patrolling many times during my night prowls, was slowly looking me up and down, making a show of trying to figure out my all-white outfit.

"Going to a pajama party?" he asked.

So much for courtesy to the public he serves, I reflected, though I'd anticipated as much. Not every policeman was a

Claude Friedrich. Friedrich might make mistakes, but he didn't mind admitting them.

"This was left on my car outside of Body Time," I said briefly, and deposited the doll on the desk in front of his feet. I'd wrapped it in a paper towel from a roll in my housekeeping kit. Now I spread the towel open.

Tom David gradually uprighted himself and put the RC Cola down. He stubbed out his cigarette, staring at the Ken doll.

"That's ugly," he said. "That's real ugly. Did you see anyone around your car?"

"No. I was in Body Time for over an hour. Anyone could have pulled into the parking lot, put the doll on my car, and pulled out without anyone seeing them. Not many people there tonight—most people don't work out on Friday evenings."

"You were at that martial arts class that Marshall Sedaka runs?"

There was something about the way he said Marshall's name . . . not just distaste but also personal dislike. I went on full alert.

"Right."

"He thinks he's tough," Tom David remarked. There was a cold light in his mean, bright eyes. "Orientals think they can order women around like they was sheep or something."

I raised my eyebrows. If anyone thought of women as interchangeable parts, it was Tom David Meiklejohn.

"Sedaka see this?"

"Yes," I said.

"He have a chance to put it on your car? You two have any personal relationship?"

"He didn't have a chance to put it on my car. He was inside Body Time when I got there, and he left after I did."

"Listen, I'm the only one here right now, and when Lottie comes back with her McNuggets, I gotta go on patrol. You want to come back in tomorrow and make a statement?"

"Okay."

"I'll try fingerprinting this, and we'll see what happens."

I nodded and turned to go. As my hand touched the door, Tom David said abruptly, "I guess you *would* be interested in self-defense."

I could feel the color draining from my face.

I looked out through the glass door into the darkness.

"Any woman should be interested in self-defense," I said, and walked out into the night.

I drove home tense with rage and fear, thinking of the bloody-eyed Ken doll, thinking of Tom David Meiklejohn mulling over what had happened to me with his buddies over a few beers. I had found the source of the leak in the police department, I was pretty sure.

I parked the car where it belonged, unlocked the back door, and threw everything but my keys and my driver's license into the house. Those I stuck in my T-shirt pocket, where they made a strange bulge over my breast. I had to walk. It was the only thing that would help.

The street was deserted at the moment. It was about 9:00 P.M. The night was much warmer than it had been the last time I walked, the humidity high, a precursor of the dreadful hot evenings of summer. It was fully dark, and I drifted into the shadows of the street, padding silently along to pass through the arboretum. Marshall's house on Farraday was not far. I didn't know the number, but I would see his car.

It relaxed me, moving through the night invisibly. I felt more like the Lily who had had a stable existence before the murder of Pardon Albee. Then, my only problem had been the sleepless nights, which came maybe twice a week; other than that, I'd had things under control.

Standing concealed in the undergrowth of the arboretum, I waited for a car to pass on Jamaica Street, so I could steal across.

I hadn't considered my route at all, but now sheer curiosity led me to drift toward the house Marshall had up until recently called home. There is very little cover on Celia Street, which is one of modest but spruce white houses with meticulously kept yards. I planned my approach. It was earlier than I usually walked, and there were more people on the move, which in Shakespeare isn't saying a hell of a lot—a car would pass occasionally, or I would see someone come out of his house, retrieve something from a pickup or jeep, and hurry back inside.

In the summer, children would be playing outside till late, but on this spring night, they all seemed to be inside.

I worked my way down the street, trying to be unobtrusive but not suspicious, since there were people still up and active. It was not a workable compromise. I'd rather be seen than reported, so I moved at a steady pace rather than drifting from one cover to another. After all, I was wearing white, hardly a camouflage color. Still, no one seemed to notice me, and curtains up and down the little street were uniformly drawn against the dark.

I only saw the police car when I was directly opposite Marshall's former home. It was parked up against Thea's next-door neighbor's hedge, which divides their yards from the street to the back of the lot. The cruiser was pulled right up behind a car that I assumed must be Thea's, which looked dark red or brown in the dim light of the streetlamp. So it didn't exactly seem the driver was paying an official visit; in fact, I concluded, Tom David Meiklejohn, whose car number 3 was parked in the driveway, was inside chitchatting with the rat-plagued Mrs. Sedaka, while he was supposed to be patrolling the streets of Shakespeare to keep them safe for widows and orphans.

Instead, it seemed Tom David Meiklejohn was personal bodyguard to one about-to-be divorcée.

I had a fleeting desire to make yet one more anonymous phone call to Claude Friedrich, before I reflected that not only would that be sneaky and dishonorable but also that a possible relationship between Thea and Tom David was none of my business.

I began moving again, ghosting silently down the dark, quiet street, thinking hard as I passed from shadow to shadow.

In five minutes, I was on Farraday. Marshall's car was parked in the gravel driveway of the house on the corner, a little house smack in the middle of a small lot needing a great deal of yard work. The rental was definitely a step down from Celia Street.

I wondered if it had been hard for Marshall to leave the Sedaka house in Thea's possession.

The porch light was glowing yellow, but I continued on through the yard and around to the back door, my eyes adapting quickly to the darkness. I rapped three times, hard, and heard Marshall's quick footsteps.

"Who's there?" he asked. He's not a man who likes surprises, either.

"Lily." He opened the door quickly. I went up the step and

into the house. And despite what he had said about having an evening of conversation, the minute the door shut, his arms went around me and his mouth found mine. My hands snaked underneath his T-shirt, eager to touch his body again.

I did not have time to marvel at my ability to have sex without fear; I did not have time to wonder if what I was doing was wise, since I carried burdens enough for two, and Marshall was not exactly an unencumbered man. But we did take a moment for protection this time, and I hoped we wouldn't pay for our previous stupidity.

Afterward, it was hard to feel the limitations of my own skin, to feel myself shrinking back into the mold in which I'd cast myself before I'd come to Shakespeare. For the first time in years, it felt confining rather than comfortable.

And yet, as I looked around Marshall's Spartan bedroom—the queen-size mattress and box spring on a frame, no headboard or footboard; a dresser clearly retrieved from someone's attic; a thrift store night table—I felt uneasy at being out of my own home. In many months, I hadn't been in anyone's house except to clean it.

We'd been lying together quietly since making love, my back to his front, his arm around me. Every now and then, Marshall would kiss my neck or stroke my side. The intimacy of the moment both excited and threatened me.

"You know Thea is seeing someone else," I said quietly.

If he wanted to get divorced, he needed to know that. If he wanted to reconcile with Thea, he needed to know that.

"I thought so," he said after a long moment. "Do you know who it is?"

"What will you do if I tell you a name?" I turned over to face him, automatically reaching down for the sheet to cover my scars. Before he answered, he took the sheet, pulled it back down, and kissed my chest.

"Don't hide from me, Lily," he whispered.

My hands twitched with the effort I was making not to grab the sheet. Marshall moved even closer to me so that his body covered the scars, and I gradually relaxed against him.

"Are you thinking I might track him down and beat him up for Thea's honor?" he asked after letting enough time pass to let me know he didn't consider Thea's affair a personal thing.

"I don't know you well enough to know what you would do."

"Thea is a hometown sweetheart, because she's pretty and she was born and bred here. She knows when to act charming and sunny. She's good with children. But the people you won't find talking about Thea with this exaggerated awe are the men she's dated for a while—the men she's dated long enough to go to bed with."

I pulled back a little to look at Marshall's face. He looked as if he had a bad taste in his mouth.

"Lily, by the time I came to town, Thea had run through the few locals she felt were worthy of her. She could tell, I think, that people were starting to wonder why pretty, sweet Thea couldn't seem to form a lasting relationship with anyone, so she dated me and married me quickly. I didn't go to bed with Thea before I married her. She said she wanted to wait and I respected that, but I found out after maybe a month, that was just because she didn't want me to back out like other men had."

"She doesn't like sex?" I asked hesitantly. I should be the

last one to criticize a woman who had problems dealing with men.

Marshall laughed in an unamused way. "Oh, no. She likes it. But she doesn't like it like we do it," and his hand ran down my back, caressed my hips. "She likes to do . . . sick things, things that hurt. Because I loved her, I tried to oblige, but it ended up making me feel bad. Sad."

Degraded, I thought.

"Then she decided she wanted a baby, and I wondered if that might save our marriage, so I tried to oblige. But I'd lost my interest by then, and . . . I couldn't." This cost Marshall a great deal to say. "So she called me names and taunted me, only in private, only when no one else could hear. Not because she cared about me, but because she didn't want anyone else to know she was capable of saying those things. Going home was like going to hell. I couldn't stand it anymore. I haven't had sex in six months, Lily, but that wasn't the worst of it, not by a long shot. So here I am, in this dump, wondering how to file for divorce without Thea taking my business away from me."

I had no response to his money worries. I have very little available cash myself because I am saving strenuously against the day when I have to have a new car, or a new roof, or any of the sudden catastrophic expenses that can wipe out a one-income household. But at least all my finances, good or bad, are dependent on me and me only. I can't imagine how I'd feel if I had to give half of my business away to someone who had found pleasure in degrading and humiliating me.

"Tom David Meiklejohn."

His eyes had been focused far away, staring past my shoulder at a bleak vista. Now he looked at me.

"The cop." His dark eyes stared into mine. I gave a tiny nod. "I'll bet she loves the handcuffs," he said.

I tried not to shrink at the thought of a woman handcuffed, but my breath came out in a little whine that drew Marshall's attention to me instantly. "Don't think of it, Lily," he said quietly. "Don't think of it; think of this." And his hand slid gently between my legs, his mouth found my breast, and I did indeed think of other things.

"Marshall," I said afterward, "if you hadn't noticed, I wanted to tell you I have absolutely no complaints about your virility." He laughed a little, breathlessly, and for a while we dozed together.

But I woke soon, anxious and ill at ease. Moving as quietly as I could, I got up and began pulling on my clothes. Marshall's breathing was still heavy and even and he shifted position, taking up more of the bed now that I wasn't in it. For a moment, I bent over the bed, my hand an inch from his shoulder. Then I drew back. I hated to wake him: I felt compelled to leave.

I eased out of the back door, punching in the button on the knob so it would lock behind me.

I'd begun thinking, as Marshall talked about Thea, of the dead rat someone had left on Thea's kitchen table in that neat white house on Celia. When I'd woken, the rat had worried me more and more.

The Ken doll, the toy handcuffs, the dead rat. Obviously, the tokens left for me referred to my past. The dead rat seemed cut from an entirely different pattern. A thought trailed through my mind like a slug: Had Thea perhaps tortured animals in her childhood? Was the rat also from Thea's past? I grimaced as I moved through the darkness. I could not bear cruelty to a helpless thing.

At this time of night, the streets were deserted, the town deep in sleep. I wasn't being as careful as I usually was. The only people likely to see me at this hour were the two patrolling policemen, and I knew where one of the two was; I'd checked on my way home, and Tom David was still at Thea's. Surely he'd gone off duty; wouldn't the dispatcher be trying to raise him otherwise?

I was yawning widely as I walked up my driveway. I'd pulled my keys from my pocket and was about to step off the drive to go to my front door when the attack came. Tired and inattentive as I'd been, I had trained for this moment for three years.

When I heard the rush of feet, I whirled to face the attacker, the keys clenched in my fist to reinforce my blow. But the man in the ski mask had a staff, maybe a mop or broom handle, and he swung it under my guard and whacked my ribs. I kept myself upright by a supreme effort, and when my assailant tried to swing the staff again, I let the keys fall, grabbed the staff with both hands, swung up my leg, and kicked him hard in the chest—not a very effective kick, but it was the best I could do under the circumstances. He did have to let go of the staff, which was good, but I staggered when he released it and dropped it myself, which was bad.

My kick had made him fall back, too, though, and that gave me time to recover my footing before he launched himself at me with a savage growl, like a dog out of control.

I was close to that point myself. When I saw the face coming toward me, shrouded in a ski mask but otherwise unguarded, I inhaled deeply, then struck as hard as I could with my fist, exhaling and locking into position automatically. The man screamed and began falling, his hands going up to clutch his nose, and on his way down, my knee came up, striking him sharply under the chin.

And that was the end of it.

Though I stood in a fighting stance in the dim light, the man was rolling and gurgling in a whipped way on my grass. Lights were coming on in the apartments—the man's scream had been piercing, if not long—and Claude Friedrich, the man used to dealing with emergencies, dashed around the dividing fence with speed rather amazing for a man of his age. His gun was drawn. I took him in at a glance, then resumed guarding the man on the grass.

Friedrich stopped short.

"What the *hell* are you doing, Lily Bard?" he asked rather breathlessly. I glanced at him again, long enough to notice that he was clad only in khaki slacks. He looked pretty good.

"This son of a bitch attacked me," I said, very pleased to hear my voice come out even.

"I would think it was the other way around, Miss Lily, if he didn't have a mask on and you weren't in your own yard."

I saw no point in responding. I kept my attention focused on the writhing, whimpering figure.

"I think he's pretty much whipped," Friedrich said, and I thought I detected a note of sarcasm. "What I really wish you would do, Lily, is go inside your little house there and call the police station and tell them I need some backup here."

What I longed to do was jump on my attacker and hit him a few more times, because the adrenaline was still pumping through my system, and by God, he had startled me. But Friedrich was making sense; there was no point in my getting into trouble. I stood straight, dropping my hands, and took a cleansing breath to relax. I took a step toward my house and felt a stab of pain, sharp enough to cause me to stop dead.

"You all right?" Friedrich said sharply, anxiously.

I found I was aching from more than the wish to punish my attacker. His first blow had been a good one, and he'd managed to rake my face with his fingers, though I couldn't remember how or when. As the rage ebbed away, the pain seeped in to take its place.

"I'll make it," I told him grimly, and reached out to pull my keys from the grass. To my dismay, the little chain had snapped and the keys had scattered under our feet. I could find only one, but at least that one was my house key. I hobbled into the house, making my way to my bedroom. I called the police station first. After I hung up, my hand stayed wrapped around the receiver. I had no idea what I'd said to the dispatcher, the unseen Lottie. It was now 1:30 in the morning.

Marshall had made me promise to call him if I had trouble.

I checked the little piece of paper he'd scrawled his new phone number on, and I punched it in.

"Yes?" Marshall asked, a little groggy but conscious.

"I'm at home, Marshall," I said.

"I knew you'd left," he said curtly.

"I had a fight."

"Are you all right?"

"Not entirely. But not as bad off as he is."

"I'm out the door."

And suddenly, I was talking to a dial tone.

I wanted more than anything else to lie down on the bed. But I knew I could not. I forced myself to get to my feet again, to move slowly back out to where Claude Friedrich was still holding a gun on "the whiner," who had covered his now-blood-soaked ski mask with both hands.

I still didn't know the identity of my attacker.

"I guess you get to pull off his mask, Lily," Friedrich said. "He can't seem to manage."

I bent painfully over, said, "Put your damn hands down," and was instantly obeyed. I grasped the edge of the ski mask with my right hand and pulled it up. It couldn't come off entirely because the back of his head pinned it down, but enough of the knit front slid up for me to recognize its wearer.

Blood slid from Norvel Whitbread's nostrils. "You done broke my nose, you bitch," he said hoarsely, and my hand snapped back to strike. Norvel cringed.

"Cut it out!" barked the chief of police, no trace of comforting rumble in his official voice, and with an effort of will, I relaxed and stepped away.

"I can smell the bourbon from here," Friedrich said disgustedly. "What were you doing when he came at you, Lily?"

"I was walking up to my own house in my own yard, minding my own business," I said pointedly.

"Oh. Like that, huh?"

"Like that," I agreed.

"Norvel, you are the stupidest son of a bitch who ever drew breath," the chief of police said conversationally.

Norvel did some moaning and groaning and then he vomited.

"Good God Almighty, man!" exclaimed Friedrich. He looked over at me. "Why you think he did this, Lily?"

"He gave me some trouble at the church the other day when I was working there, so I thumped him," I said flatly. "This is his idea of revenge, I guess." Norvel seemed to stick to tools of his trade when he planned an assault. I was willing to bet the staff was the same broom he'd tried to hit me with at the church, with the straw sawed off.

A city police car came around the corner, lights rotating but siren silent, which was something to be thankful for.

A thought struck me and I squatted a few feet away from Norvel, who now smelled of many unpleasant things. "Listen, Norvel, did you leave that doll on my car tonight?" I asked.

Norvel Whitbread responded with a stream of abuse and obscenity, the burden of which was that he didn't know what I meant.

"What's that about?" asked Friedrich.

"Okay, let's try again, Norvel," I said, struck by a sudden inspiration. I held up a wait-a-minute hand to Friedrich. "Why did Tom O'Hagen go upstairs to see you the day Pardon was killed?"

"Because he couldn't keep his dick in his pants," snarled Norvel, in no mood to keep anyone else's potentially lucrative secret any longer. "He gave me sixty lousy bucks not to tell his wife he's been screwing Deedra."

Claude Friedrich was standing closer now. He'd moved in imperceptibly when he heard my question. Now he exploded in a cold kind of anger. "Little something you forgot to mention to me, Norvel?" he asked furiously. "When we get you into a cell after a side trip to the hospital, we're going to have a serious conversation." He nodded to the deputy who'd trotted over from the patrol car, a young man I mentally classified as a boy.

While the deputy handcuffed Norvel and inserted him into the patrol car, Claude Friedrich stood by my side and stared down at me. I was still squatting, just because I knew getting up was going to hurt pretty bad. Tucking his gun in his waistband, Friedrich extended a hand. After a moment's hesitation, I reached up to grasp it, and he pulled hard. I rose with a gasp.

"No point asking you where you've been—well, maybe I don't need to," he said, eyeing Marshall's car as it pulled in behind the patrol car. He let go of my hand, which he'd retained.

Marshall launched himself out of his car with gratifying speed. He did not grab me or hug me; he looked me over carefully, as if he was scrutinizing a piece of sale furniture for scratches and dents.

"We need to go inside," he muttered. "I can't see well enough out here."

Claude Friedrich stirred. "Mr. Sedaka, good evenin'," he said.

Marshall looked at him for the first time. "Chief," he acknowledged, with a brief nod, before going back to his scrutiny of my facial scratches. "Her face is bleeding," he informed Friedrich, "and I need to take her in and clean the cuts up so I can see their depth."

I felt a sudden urge to giggle. I hadn't been examined this carefully since my mother had gotten a letter from the school about head lice.

"Norvel Whitbread attacked Lily," observed the older man, who was beginning to feel the cool air against his bare chest, judging from the goose pimples I could see popping up. Friedrich seemed determined to push Marshall into acting like a proper boyfriend, perhaps consoling me on my ordeal and threatening death to Norvel.

"I'm assuming you whipped his butt," Marshall told me.

"Yes, sensei," I said, and suddenly the giggle burst out.

Both men stared at me in such complete amazement that I giggled all the harder, and then shook with laughter.

"Maybe she should go to the hospital along with Norvel?"

"Oh, he has to go to the hospital?" Marshall was as proud as if his much-coached Little Leaguer had hit a home run.

"Broke his nose," I confirmed between the sporadic giggles that marked the wind-down of my fit.

"He armed?"

"Broomstick, I think," I said. "It's over there." The staff had landed in the low shrubs around my front porch.

Friedrich went over to retrieve it. Evidence, I assumed.

"Lily," he rumbled, carrying the wood gingerly by one end, "you're gonna have to come in tomorrow and make a statement. I won't make you come in tonight. It's late and you need some attention. I'm prepared to take you to the hospital if you want."

"No thank you," I said soberly, completely over my mirth. "I really want to go into my house." More than anything, I was realizing, I wanted a shower. I'd had my usual workday, then karate class, two longish walks, sex, and a fight. I felt, and surely was, pretty gamy.

"Then I'll leave you to it," Friedrich said quietly. "I'm glad you came out on the good side. And I'm assuming when I go into the station I'll find out what this is about a doll left on your car?"

I could not forbear raising my eyebrows significantly in Marshall's direction. It was lucky my good sense had propelled me to the police station earlier in the evening. Marshall glared at me. I smiled back. "Yes, sir," I said, trying not to sound smug. "I reported it earlier, to Tom David Meiklejohn. He wanted me to come in tomorrow and make a statement, too."

"You got jobs on Saturday morning?"

"Yes, I do, but I'll be in at noon, anyway."

"I'll see you then. Good night to you both." And the policeman strode off, carrying the broom handle.

With his departure, my exhaustion hit me in the face.

"Let's go in," I said. I scanned the grass, dimly lit by the streetlights at the corners of the arboretum. My key ring had broken. Luckily, the broken key ring was my personal one, with only my house, car, and lockbox key on it. I spotted a gleam of metal in the grass—my car key. Without thinking, I bent to retrieve it and felt a ripple of pain in the side that had taken the brunt of the first blow. I gave a little hiss of shock, and Marshall, who'd been staring after the departing lawman, helped me straighten.

I spotted my lockbox key on the way to the porch, and Marshall retrieved it for me. He helped me up the steps and into the house. Until I saw him look around, I had forgotten he'd never been in it.

He said, "We need the bathroom," and waved me into preceding him. Marshall undressed me quite . . . clinically. First, he cleaned the scratches on my face, put antibiotic ointment on them, and then he turned his attention to my ribs. He ran his fingers over each rib, gently but firmly, asking me questions as his fingers evaluated my injury.

"Take two aspirin and call me in the morning," he said finally. "I don't think anything's broken. But you'll have a bad bruise and you'll be sore. I'll tape you. It's lucky he's a sedentary alcoholic, or you'd be in the hospital now. How much warning did you have?"

"Not as much as I should have," I admitted. "He was waiting for me in the carport, with the mask and dark clothes on. But still . . ." and my voice trailed off, as I found I could not put one coherent thought together. He got my first-aid kit from the little linen closet and worked on me for a while.

"I have to shower," I said. "Out."

"Keep the tape dry. Turn that side away from the water.

"Yes, sensei."

"I'm sleeping on your couch tonight."

"It's a love seat. You'll get cramped."

"Sleeping bag?"

"Nope. Don't like camping."

"Floor."

"You can sleep with me. It's queen-sized."

I could tell he wanted to ask me why I'd left his bed earlier in the night. I was glad he was too decent to badger me when I was so exhausted. He helped me off with the rest of my clothes and then just left, without saying a word. I felt immense gratitude and relief. I turned on the shower and as soon as the water ran warm enough, I stepped in, pulled the curtain closed, and just let the water run over me. After a few seconds, I got the soap and shampoo and made as thorough a job of it as I could with Marshall's strictures. I even shaved under my arms, though bending over for my legs was too difficult.

When I stepped out into the steamy room and brushed my teeth, I felt much more like myself. My nightgown was hanging on the hook on the back of the door, and I pulled it over my head after my automatic deodorant, skin cream, and cuticle remover routine. I'd almost forgotten Marshall was there until I went in my bedroom. It was a shock to see the black hair on the pillow next to mine. He'd civilly taken the inside of the bed and left me the outside by the night table, and he'd left the bedside lamp switched on. He was sound asleep, on his left side, turned away from me.

Moving as silently as I could, I checked the front and back doors and all the windows—my nightly routine—and turned off the lamp. I slid into bed cautiously, turned on my right side, my unbandaged side, so my back was to his, and despite the strangeness of having someone in my house and bed, I was sucked down into sleep like water circling around the drain in my sink.

My eyes flew open at eight o'clock. The digital clock on the bedside table was right in front of me. I tried to think what was so different. . . . Then I remembered the night before. My back felt very warm; it was pressed against Marshall's. Then I felt him move behind me, and his arm wrapped around my chest. My nightgown was thin and I could feel him pressing against me.

"How are you?" he asked quietly.

"Haven't moved yet," I murmured back.

"Want to move some?"

"You have something specific in mind?" I asked as I felt his body respond to contact with me.

"Only if it won't hurt you. . . ."

I arched harder against him and felt him press against me fiercely in response.

"We'll just have to try it out, see if it hurts," I whispered.

"You sure?"

I turned over to face him. "Sure," I said.

His strength enabled him to hold his weight off me, and

his eyes showed nothing but pleasure. In view of my scratched face and the black bruises on my side, I found this touching and amazing. I realized I'd already gotten used to his acceptance of the scars. So it was doubly dismaying to me, after we had finished lovemaking and were lying side by side holding hands, when he said, "Lily, I've got to talk to you about something." His voice was serious, too serious.

I felt my heart shrivel.

"What?" I asked, trying to sound casual. I pulled the sheet up.

"It's your quads, Lily."

"My . . . *quadriceps?*" I said incredulously.

"You really need to work on them," Marshall told me.

I turned to stare at him. "I have scars all over my abdomen, I have scratches across my face, I have a huge bruise on my ribs, and your only remark about my body is that I need to work on my quads?"

"You're perfect except for your quads."

"You . . . jerk!" Torn between amusement and disbelief, I pulled the pillow from under my head and hit him with it, which immediately activated the pain. I couldn't hold back my exclamation of dismay, and clapped my hand to my side.

"Lean back," Marshall urged me, sitting up to help. "Lean back, slowly . . . there. Raise your head a little." He slid my pillow back under my head.

"Lily," he said when he could tell the worst had passed. "Lily, I was teasing."

"Oh." I felt abruptly and totally like a fool.

"Well, I guess I'm hardly social anymore," I said after a moment.

"Lily. Why'd you leave last night?"

"I just felt restless. I'm not used to sharing time, or space, with anyone. I'm not used to visiting people's homes as a guest. You're still married. You're used to having someone else around. Probably you and Thea were invited places, right? But I'm not. I don't date. I'm just . . ." I hesitated, not sure how to characterize my life of the past few years.

"Coasting?"

I considered. "Existing," I said. "Going from day to day safely. Doing my work, paying my way, not attracting any attention. Left alone."

"Not lonely?"

"Not often," I admitted. "There are not that many people I like or have respect for, so I hardly want their company."

Marshall was propped up on one elbow, his muscular chest a treat for my eyes. And I thought of it that way, as a treat: a seldom-achieved, rare thing that might not happen again. "Who do you like?" he asked me.

I thought about it. "I like Mrs. Hofstettler. I like Claude Friedrich, I think, in spite of everything. I like you. I like most of the people in the karate class, though I'm not partial to Janet Shook. I like the new doctor, the woman. But I don't know any of those people that well."

"Do you have any friends you don't know through work or karate class, anyone your own age that you . . . go shopping with, go to eat in Little Rock with?"

"No," I said, my voice flat and verging on anger.

"Okay, okay." He raised a placating hand. "I'm just asking. I want to know how uphill this is going to be."

"Pretty uphill, I'm afraid." I relaxed with an effort. I glanced at the clock again. "Marshall, I don't want to leave, but I have to work."

"Are you just having a flash of antisocializing, or do you really have to work this morning?"

"I really have to work. I have to clean the doctor's office this morning, visit Mrs. Hofstettler, go to the police station, and do my own shopping this afternoon." I keep grocery expenses down by making a careful list and following it to the letter on my one visit to the grocery store a week.

"How are you going to manage with your ribs?"

"I'll just do what I have to do," I said with some surprise. "It's my job. If I don't work, I don't get paid. If I don't get paid, I go down the drain."

"I have to open up the gym, too," he said reluctantly. "At least it opens late on Saturday, but I don't have anyone to work until one today, so I do have to get there."

"We have to start moving," I suggested, but I was suddenly reluctant to crawl out of the warm bed with its odor of him and sex.

"Can I take you out to supper tonight?"

I had that pressed feeling again. I almost balked, said no. But I told myself sternly that I'd be cutting my own throat. Marshall was throwing out a lifeline and I was refusing to grasp it.

"Sure," I said, aware that I sounded stiff and anxious.

Marshall studied me.

"You pick the place," he suggested. "What do you like?"

I had not eaten in a restaurant in longer than I cared to add up. On nights I decide I don't want to cook, which isn't that often, since I enjoy cooking and it is cheaper than eating out, I pick up food and bring it home.

"Um," I said, drawing on an old memory, "I like Mexican food."

"Great, so do I. We'll go to El Paso Grande in Montrose."

Montrose was the nearest large town to Shakespeare, and the one where Shakespeare residents did most of their shopping when they didn't want to drive the hour and a half to Little Rock.

"All right." I carefully sat up and swung my legs over the side of the bed. I bit my lip and I stayed there, trying to feel like getting up and brushing my teeth. I wanted Marshall to ignore my struggle, and miraculously he did, letting me take my time and rise on my own, then walk stiffly to the bathroom for a quick sponge bath and a meticulous brushing of my teeth and hair. I applied makeup quickly and thoroughly, hoping the scratches would be less conspicuous. I turned my face from side to side, checking it in the mirror, and decided I looked much better.

But I still looked just like a woman who'd been in a fight.

I walked out, still holding myself stiffly upright, to let Marshall have his turn.

By the time he emerged, having showered and used a toothbrush in a plastic wrapper I'd put out for him on my sink (the dentist gives me a new one every time he cleans my teeth, but it is a brand I don't like), I'd managed to dress myself in the cheap clothes I wore to work: loose-leg blue jeans and an old dark red college sweatshirt with lopped-off arms. I hadn't been able to cope with pulling on socks, so I'd slid my feet into loafers instead of my usual cross-trainers.

Marshall started to speak, stopped, thought the better of it, and finally settled with saying, "Pick you up at six?"

I approved of his skipping all the "Are you sure you can do it? Why don't you call in sick today? Let me help you" stuff I'd been afraid he was going to put us through.

"Sure," I said, showing him gratitude with my smile.

"See you then," he said briefly, and went out to his car, which was still parked rather crookedly in front of the house.

Moving slowly but keeping going, I gathered together what I needed for the day and drove over to the doctor's office. As usual, I parked in the paved area behind the building, intended for the doctor and staff. I noticed without much interest that Dr. Thrush's car was there, too. Dr. Thrush is new in town and I had just started cleaning for her three weeks ago.

I used my key and stepped uncomfortably over the high threshold. Carrie Thrush was sticking her head out of her office, her brows drawn together with anxiety.

"Oh, thank goodness it's you, Lily!" the doctor exclaimed. "I forgot it was time for you to come." Then, as I moved down the hall, the relieved smile gave way to concern. "Good God, woman, what happened to you?"

"I had a fight last night," I said.

"In a bar?" The young doctor looked amazed, her dark brown eyebrows raised above eyes just as dark and brown.

"No, a guy jumped me in my yard," I said briefly, explaining only because she'd asked with so much concern.

I didn't have much energy to spare today, so I had to focus on the job at hand. I opened the door of the patients' bathroom in the hall. That was the worst place, so that was where I always started. I had a strong feeling that between my own scheduled cleaning times, Dr. Thrush came in every morning and gave it a light going-over herself. That bathroom would be even dirtier otherwise. I pulled on my gloves and started in.

I cleaned the little double-doored space where patients put their urine samples, then wiped off the knob of the little door

into the lab. I laid a fresh paper towel down for the next patient's sample. I remembered I hadn't tested this pair of rubber gloves for leaks, and reminded myself to do that when I
got home. The last thing I needed was to catch a bug here.

I became aware that Dr. Thrush was standing in the bathroom doorway staring at me.

"You surely can't work in that condition!" Carrie Thrush
said.

She has a firm voice that I believe she'd assume to keep
people mindful she is indeed a doctor. Carrie Thrush is shorter
than I am and pigeon-plump. She has a round face with a determined jaw, unplucked eyebrows, and acne scars. She wears
her chin-length black hair parted and brushed back behind
her ears. Her dark brown eyes are round and clear, all that saves
the doctor from plainness. I set her age at about my own, early
thirties.

"Well, yes I can," I said, since she was waiting for a response. I was not in the mood for arguing. I sprinkled pow-
dered cleanser in the sink and wet the sponge to scour it. I
compressed my lips in what I hoped was a determined line.

"Could I just look at your ribs? That's your problem, right?
Listen, you're in a doctor's office."

I kept on scrubbing, but my good sense conquered my
pride. I laid down the sponge, pulled off my gloves, and pulled
up my shirt.

"Oh, someone taped you, I see. Well, let me just take this
off. . . ." I had to endure all the probing again, to hear a bona
fide doctor tell me just as Marshall had that none of my ribs
were broken but that the bruise and pain would last for a
while. Of course Carrie Thrush saw the scars, and her lips
pursed, but she didn't ask any questions.

"You shouldn't be working," the doctor said. "But I can tell that nothing I could say would stop you, so work away."

I blinked. That was refreshing. I began to like Carrie Thrush more and more.

Cleaning the Shakespeare Clinic was an exasperating task because of paper. Paper was the curse of the doctor's office. Forms in triplicate, billing forms, patient health histories, reports from labs, insurance forms, Medicare, Medicaid—they were stacked everywhere. I had to respect each stack as an entity, lift it to dust and put it down in the same spot; so the office shared by the receptionist and the clerk was in and of itself a land mine. Compared with the office, the waiting room and examining rooms were cakewalks.

For the first time, it struck me that someone must also be cleaning those more often than once a week. As I vacuumed, I mulled this thought over. Nita Tyree, the receptionist? I couldn't picture Nita agreeing to that as part of her job. I barely know Nita, but I do know she has four children, two of whom are young enough to be in day care at SCC. So Nita leaves when the last patient walks out the front door, no matter what is sitting on her desk.

Gennette Jinks, the nurse, was out of the picture. I'd been behind the fiftyish Gennette in line at the Superette Food Mart only the week before and had heard (as had everone else in a five-foot radius) about how hard it was to work for a woman, how young Dr. Thrush wasn't accepting the wisdom she (Gennette) had attained with years of experience, at which point I had tuned out and read the headlines on the tabloids instead, since they had more entertainment value.

So the surreptitious weekday cleaner had to be the good doctor herself. I had stacked up the bills. Without wanting to,

I knew how much Carrie Thrush still owed for her education, and I had a feeling that some weeks it was hard for Carrie to pay even me, much less Gennette and Nita.

I chewed this over as I mopped, having dusted and vacuumed around the doctor as she sat at her desk, a stack of the omnipresent paper on every available inch of surface.

When I had everything gleaming and smelling at least clean, if not sweet, I stuck my head in the office door and said, "Good-bye."

"Oh, let me write you a check," said Dr. Thrush.

"No."

"What?" Carrie Thrush paused, her pen touching her checkbook.

"No. You examined me. Call it bartering."

I was sure that was against some doctors' rules, but I was also sure the offer would appeal to my employer. And I was right. Carrie Thrush smiled broadly, then said, "Thank God! No paper to fill out."

"Thank God, no insurance to file," I answered, and left, feeling that Carrie Thrush and I, cleaning woman and doctor, had, if not a relationship, at least the beginning of good feelings between us.

Nine

My bruised side ached more and more as Saturday dragged by. I moved through Mrs. Hofstettler's apartment like a snail, but she was having one of her bad days and didn't seem to notice. I wondered what it would be like to feel this way many days and to know for a certainty it would last the rest of my life.

I made my statement at the police station, sitting bolt upright and taking shallow breaths. The man who took it down was a detective, I had to assume, since he wasn't wearing a uniform. He told me he was Dolph Stafford and that he was mighty glad to meet me. He glanced at me out the corners of his eyes, and I saw pity in his elaborate courtesy. I knew he, too, had heard my old story, which I dragged around with me wherever I went, like the albatross around the Ancient Mariner's neck.

As I drearily went through the details of the Ken doll and Norvel's attack, I pondered an old problem. Now that my past was out, should I move? Before, the answer had always been yes. But I'd been in Shakespeare for four years now, longer than I'd been anywhere since I was raped. For the first time, I wondered if I might not just weather it out. The thought crossed my mind, and in crossing, it stuck there. When Dolph Stafford dismissed me, I went home to lie down, finally giving in to the pain. I'd just have to go grocery shopping Sunday or Monday.

My reluctance to go to the store wasn't wholly due to the pain. I knew by now the story about Norvel's attack would be all over town, and I just didn't want to encounter sympathetic looks or horrified questions.

Carrie Thrush had slipped me a few sample pain pills when I'd left her office. Normally, I'd think twice before taking Tylenol, but I was positively longing for whatever relief the pills might bring.

Swallowing two of the capsules with some water, I was just about to leave the kitchen to ease myself onto the bed when I heard someone knocking at the door.

I nearly decided to ignore it. But it was the brisk kind of rap-rap-rap that tells you that the caller is both impatient and persistent. I was already peeved when I got to the door and looked through the peephole, so discovering the caller was my sometime employer the Reverend Joel McCorkindale did not make me any happier. I shot back the bolt reluctantly.

The minister's "happy to see you, sister" smile faltered as he took in the scratches on my face and the awkward way I was standing.

"May I come in?" He was wisely settling for dignified sympathy.

"Briefly."

Taking that in his stride, McCorkindale stepped across the threshold and surveyed my tiny domain.

"Very nice," he said with great sincerity. I reminded myself I must be careful. Sincerity was the Reverend McCorkindale's middle name.

I didn't offer him a chair.

This, too, he absorbed without comment.

"Miss Bard," he began when he'd taken measure of my attitude, "I know that you and Norvel Whitbread have had a personality conflict"—here I snorted—"ever since you've had to work together at the church. I want you to know I'm extremely disturbed that he was so stupid last night, and I want you to know Norvel himself is very, very sorry he frightened you so badly."

I had been looking down, wondering when he'd get through blathering, because my bed seemed to have acquired a voice and it was calling me louder and louder. But now I looked up at Joel McCorkindale.

"I was never frightened," I said. "Mad, yes. But not frightened."

"Well, that's . . . good. Then, he's apologetic for having hurt you."

"I beat the shit out of him."

The minister flushed. "He is definitely a sad sight today."

I smiled.

"So, cut to the chase," I prompted.

"I have come to ask you, most humbly, if you would consider dropping the charges against Norvel. He is repentant. He knows he should not have been drinking. He knows it is wrong, very wrong, to hold grudges. He knows it is against God's commandments to harm another person, much less a woman."

I closed my eyes, wondering if he'd ever listened to himself.

The bad thing was, I reflected as McCorkindale expanded on Norvel's mental anguish, that if I hadn't had my little life-altering experience, I might be tempted to listen to this crap.

I held up a hand, indicating for him to stop.

"I am going to prosecute him to the full extent of the law," I said flatly. "I don't care if you ever hire me again. You've known he was drinking again for weeks; you had to have known. You know whatever convictions he expresses are going to vanish when he sees another bottle. That's his religion. I have never been able to understand why you kept him on when that became apparent to anyone who cared to look. Maybe he has something on you. I don't know and I don't care. But I will not drop charges."

He took this well, like the shrewd man he is. He looked off to one side thoughtfully, turning something over in his mind.

"Lily, I have to tell you some members of our little church have felt the same way about you. They've wondered why I haven't let you go. You know, Lily, you're not everybody's cup of tea."

I felt an intense desire to laugh. The medication was undoubtedly kicking in.

"You're a mysterious and violent woman," McCorkindale prodded further. "Some people have wondered out loud to me if you should still be working in Shakespeare, or at least at our little church."

"I don't care if I work at your little church or not," I said. "But I'll tell you, if I catch you pressuring my employers to fire me because I'm 'mysterious and violent,' I'll sue you. Anyone who cares to can look up my past. And as for violent, present me with a list of fights I've started, or times I've been in jail, and I'll be real interested to read it."

Ashamed of myself for offering even that much defense of charges that were indefensible, I waved the minister out of the door and locked it firmly behind him.

My bed was screaming now, and I never could ignore a

scream. I floated down the hall and didn't even register the painful process of lying down.

When I woke up, there was a note on my bedside table.

I'd have to admit, were the Reverend McCorkindale to chance by, that this *did* scare me.

It was from Marshall.

"I came by at six to take you to supper in Montrose," the note began, in Marshall's tiny angular handwriting. "I knocked for five minutes, and then you came to the door. You let me in, walked back to your bed, got in, and went back to sleep. I was worried till I found the little envelope with 'For Pain' written on it. Call me when you wake up. Marshall."

I read it over twice while I recovered from my flash of fear.

I looked at the clock. It read 5:00. Hmm. I rolled over somewhat gingerly to exit the other side of the bed. I peered between the blind slats. Black outside. It was five in the morning.

"God Almighty," I said, impressed with Dr. Thrush's medicine. I took a few steps around the room, and I was pleased to discover that I felt much better after my long rest. The worst of the soreness seemed to be gone. It worried me that I'd let Marshall in. Had I known it was Marshall? Would I have let just anybody in? If so, it was lucky that no one else had knocked. Or had they?

Suddenly anxious, I went through the whole house. Everything was exactly as it had been the day before; the only addition was Marshall's note and the pill envelope, still containing two capsules.

After I stowed the remaining pain pills away with great

respect, I made some coffee and wondered what to do with the day. Sunday is my day off, not because it is a church day, but because it is the least desirable day of the week to clean, from my clients' standpoint. And I feel I deserve one whole day off every week. Usually, I clean my own house or mow my lawn in the morning. When Body Time opens at one, I walk in the doors. I often stay for two hours, then come home to cook for the week. I rent movies from Rainbow Video ("Cinema across the Spectrum"), and every once in a while I call my parents.

Since I'd risen so early, and since all week had been unusual, somehow none of this sounded appealing at all.

After I had skimmed through my big Sunday Little Rock paper, treading my difficult reading path around stories of battered wives, neglected children, and starving, abandoned elders to arrive at those I could actually read (which pretty much boiled down to escaped dangerous pets—this week a boa constrictor—politics, and sports), I dressed in a gingerly way, hoping the bending wouldn't wake up my side. To my pleasure, the terrible ache did not return; there was a certain amount of tenderness, and leaning in some directions was painful, but nothing nearly as bad as it had been the day before.

All right, then. I'd just quell these rebellious feelings I had, this discontent.

My house needed cleaning.

I put on my rubber gloves with what was very nearly pleasure. It crossed my mind to call Marshall, or to drift through the dawn to his house and share his bed again. But I put those thoughts aside; I was in danger of counting on him, of thinking of my life as substantially changed. I found myself wistfully staring at my gloves and thinking of the pleasures of sex with Marshall, of the wonders of his body, of the excitement of being desirable.

But I began serious cleaning.

It is a small house, which never gets very dirty anyway, and I know it very well. In an hour and a half, by the time the rest of the world was waking up, my house shone and I was looking forward to a shower.

The quiet tap on the back door came as I was about to step in. With a curse, I wrapped my white terry robe back around myself and padded quietly to the door. I looked through the peephole. Marshall looked back. I sighed, not knowing if I was glad to see him or sorry that he kept raising my expectations. I unlocked the door.

"If you don't stop this," I said flatly, "I'll think you really like me."

"Hi to you, too," he said, his eyebrows arching in surprise. "Are you conscious this time?"

"Why don't you get in the shower with me," I said over my shoulder as I went back to my hot running water, "and find out?"

As it turned out, I was fully conscious.

As he kissed me while the water ran over us, I had a terrifying feeling that I wanted to save this moment, that it was precious. I knew the fallacy inherent in planning on anything lasting, I knew the degradation I'd undergone had altered me permanently, and I was afraid.

Afterward, I loaned him my terry robe and I put on my bright, thin one, and we watched an old movie on cable together. I put a bowl of grapes between us on the love seat, we put up the footrest, and we had a pleasant time appreciating the actors and laughing at the plot. When the movie ended close to noon, I got up to return the grapes to the refrigerator. Through the open blinds of the living room window, I observed a vaguely familiar red car driving by very slowly.

"Who's that, Marshall?" I asked sharply, the outside world coming back with a rush.

He was on his feet quickly and stared out the window.

"That's Thea," he said. His voice was tight with controlled fury.

"She's driven by other times." It was the car that had passed the day Marshall was kissing me in the carport. I'd seen it several times over the past few days.

"Shit, Lily," he said, "I'm sorry. I wish the divorce had already gone through. No judge would believe, with her sitting there looking so southern belle, what she's capable of."

I was still staring out of the window, lost in thought, when the Yorks walked by. Alvah and T. L. were holding hands, moving rather slowly, and wearing everyday clothes. They were missing church, an unheard-of occurrence.

But I was not as amazed as I might have been days ago. This past week had been full of atypical behavior on the part of almost everyone I knew, including myself.

Pardon had somehow talked himself into getting killed.

The upright, churchgoing Yorks had been derailed by the rape of their granddaughter.

Norvel Whitbread had shown his true colors after two years of being smarmy.

Tom O'Hagen had cheated on Jenny O'Hagen.

Deedra Deane had seen a dead body.

Claude Friedrich had been careless with a report.

Carlton Cockroft had exercised and revealed a wholly unexpected interest in his neighbor.

Marcus Jefferson had gotten to entertain his son in his own apartment.

Marie Hofstettler had had an interview with the police.

The Reverend Joel McCorkindale had visited me in my home.

Marshall Sedaka had taken a personal interest in one of his students.

One of his students had taken a personal interest right back.

Someone had rolled a body into the arboretum.

Someone else had deposited handcuffs where I would find them; killed a rat; left a painted Ken doll on my car hood.

"Overall," I said, turning to Marshall, "it would be hard to top last week."

"We can give it a shot," he suggested, and was surprised when I laughed.

"Let me tell you what happened last Monday night," I said, and for the first time I told Marshall what I'd seen when I was out walking.

"You saw the murderer?"

"I saw the person dumping the body."

Marshall thought my story over. "I can understand why you didn't want to tell the police," he said finally. "With your cart being used. And since they didn't arrest anyone yet, you might be putting yourself in danger."

"How so?"

"The killer might think you had seen more than you actually saw," Marshall said. "At least, killers always do in the movies.

They're always coming after the person they think knows something, whether or not it's true."

"Yeah, but that's the movies. This is Shakespeare."

I suddenly realized what I'd said and I laughed. Marshall looked at me warily; I had to explain.

"Lily, I think the sooner the police arrest someone for this, the better it'll be for you."

"No argument there."

"Then we can concentrate on finding out who's playing these tricks on you and Thea."

There was something in his voice that alerted me. "Has something else happened to her?" I asked.

"She called me about six this morning. Someone came to the back door and spray-painted 'Bitch' across it."

"Is that so." Marshall looked a little surprised at my lack of horror.

"So, Marshall, did you come over here to enjoy my company or to see if I was gonna walk back up in my yard with a spray can in my hand?"

Marshall closed his eyes and took a deep breath. "Lily, I think if you were mad at Thea, you would challenge her to fight, or ignore her for the rest of your life. I can't imagine you sneaking around in the dark spray-painting a woman's back door."

But I wasn't so sure he believed that down to his bones. Hadn't there been a moment, a flicker, of something else—of relief—when I challenged him?

I sank down in the armchair and looked at him intently. "I don't know if I'm at fault, if I'm being overly prickly, or if Thea has undermined your confidence in your own judgment so much that you can't trust your own instincts."

Marshall was not quick to respond, and I was glad. I wanted him to think about this.

"Maybe both," he said finally. "Come on, it's almost time to work out."

As I pulled on my ancient gray sweatpants and a dark blue T-shirt, I pondered the fact that he was quite willing to have sex with me even though he hadn't exactly given me a rousing vote of confidence. Did that mean he was so delighted with his returned virility that he just didn't care whether I was tormenting his wife?

Dealings between men and women are all too often like picking through a minefield, I thought with some disgust. Marshall was out in the living room waiting for me. He'd walked over in workout clothes, blue sweatpants and a maroon Body Time T-shirt.

It was strange that I could stand in the hall and watch Marshall stretch that wonderful body and feel a wave of lust, that I could love the way he didn't flinch at the horrible story I'd told him. But still, I drew back from him from time to time.

This was one of the times.

We didn't talk much on the way to Body Time in my car, but the prospect of doing something I enjoyed with Marshall, who also enjoyed it, made me feel more relaxed.

Janet Shook was on the treadmill when we entered. Her eyes widened. She clearly was adding two and two in her head. I waved casually. Marshall exchanged a few words with Derrick, who'd opened for him, and then we mapped out our workout. It was legs day—not my favorite—but even doing legs was not so bad with company.

It was very convenient and pleasant having Marshall there

to take the weights on and off and spot for me; it was equally pleasant being able to return the favor.

People who before had only nodded to me came up to speak, since I was with Marshall. Of course, everyone knew him. And I found that they knew who I was, too: They all called me Lily. Though my scratched face got some sideways glances, no one mentioned Norvel Whitbread.

This, too, was pleasant, but I found that after greetings had been exchanged, I had nothing to say. I just listened as they chatted with Marshall. Marshall is a kind of community clearing house. Everyone who approached him had some piece of gossip or news to relate and seemed to feel free to speak in front of me. I wondered why.

I found, as the second gossiper in a row referred to it, that I had a reputation for being closemouthed. It surprised me to think that people thought of me at all, but I should have remembered: In small towns, there is no such thing as an invisible life.

Despite twinges in my side, I had finished leg-pressing three hundred pounds when Brian Gruber, an executive at the mattress-manufacturing plant that was one of Shakespeare's larger employers, drifted by in the course of his workout to murmur quietly in Marshall's ear. Marshall listened grimly, doing a lot of curt nodding. This was so definitely a man-to-man talk that I did an extra set so they could finish. After all, Marshall had said my quads needed work.

When I was through, I just lay there and panted. Brian wandered away to do bicep curls while Marshall added a twenty-five to each side of the leg press for his set, looking thoughtful and grim. He didn't meet my eyes as I made way for him. I reached for my sweat towel and began dabbing at my forehead.

Damned if I was going to ask.

Marshall slid into position. He put his feet up on the push board, aligned them carefully. He pushed a little, taking the pressure off the relief bars, which he flipped to the side simultaneously. Then he bared his teeth in a snarl of effort and began his set. Maybe he was trying to make me feel equal; three hundred was my top weight, and I knew Marshall could do double that. I waited stonily till his set was over and he'd flipped the bars back into place. He beckoned to me to crouch down where he lay.

So, here came the bad news.

"Brian just heard that Thea's been telling everyone at her church that she's going to put me through the wringer as far as property goes. But he also told me the same thing you did—that she's been having overnight company, which'll count against her in court."

"You've been having company, too." I watched his face go blank.

I stood up and covered my face with the towel as though I was bathed in sweat, when in fact I'd cooled down. I had to get my indifferent face back on. I felt a strong inclination to pick up my workout bag and leave without a word, but that would be cowardly.

I shifted so my back was to the leg press, and I stared at a pretty teenager who was having the time of her life showing Bobo Winthrop how hard it was for her to bench-press two ten-pound dumbbells. Bobo looked over at me, his eyes widening as he took in my marred face. His mouth formed the words *You okay?* I nodded. Then the girl on the bench said something to claim his attention. I looked in another direction so Bobo wouldn't meet my eyes again and feel obliged to come over to talk to me.

I felt hands on my shoulders, and I twitched like a horse trying to dislodge a fly.

"So, I'll just have to find some other toehold," Marshall said calmly. He began to take off the twenty-fives he'd added.

"Leave them on," I said. I slid into position, braced my feet, flipped the braces to the side, and began to push.

I managed five reps before I could tell that serious pain was just around the corner.

To finish up, we did three sets, thirty each, of lunges and leg lifts in the aerobics room. When we sat up after a short rest, I said what I thought he was waiting for me to say. "I don't think we should see each other until you're really divorced. Thea is unstable; she's in trouble at work and at home. There's no point making things worse for her, which will only make it worse for you in the long run—your property settlement and all."

"I don't want a sick woman like that dictating what my life will be like," Marshall said. He meant it, but he was also relieved. I could hardly blame him; I'd worked hard for what I had, too.

"Then there's the trick-playing thing," I went on after a calculated pause. "I can't go on being scared every time I step out of my house that someone's going to put something on my doorstep or leave something on my car. Maybe if we don't see each other for a while, that'll let up. If it's the same person who's playing tricks on Thea, it's someone who has serious feelings about you; maybe he, or she, will let you know about those feelings if I'm not around. You can deal with it, and I'll be clear of it."

"I don't know what to say, Lily," Marshall said. "I don't want to lose you now that we finally . . ."

"I'm not going anywhere," I said, and got to my feet, ignoring the reawakened pain in my side. "We'll see each other in karate class, and here sometimes." I left before Marshall had to think of something else to say.

As I drove home, I became aware that I was feeling something I hadn't felt in years: disappointment.

No sooner had I turned the corner to Track Street than I saw the police car at the curb outside my house. Leaning against it was Claude Friedrich, as solid and immovable as if he had all the time in the world.

I made a sudden decision to go grocery shopping, and after checking the traffic behind me, I backed up before Friedrich could see me and reversed my direction in a convenient driveway. I didn't want to talk to anyone right now, least of all the all-too-perceptive Friedrich.

I hadn't been to the store without a list in years. Sunday is the day I usually cook ahead, and my little freezer was almost empty.

The last time I'd been in Kroger's, I'd been shopping for myself and for the return of the Yorks. . . . Hey, they'd never reimbursed me for the groceries, or for the work I'd done last Wednesday. I hated the thought of bothering them, knowing how devastated they were by the trial of their granddaughter's assailant, but if they felt better to the extent of being able to take a walk, they could pay me.

I was trying to remember all the ingredients of my favorite tortilla casserole when a cart slammed into mine. I looked up sharply and realized the anger rolling around inside me had found an excellent focus, here to my left, wearing a modest shirtwaist dress and loafers.

The woman pushing the other cart was Thea Sedaka. Thea had bumped my cart on purpose; the stare she fixed on me aimed at contrite but never made it past loathing.

It had been a long time since I'd seen Thea this close. She was as pretty as ever. Tiny and small-boned, the future ex-Mrs. Sedaka has a sweet oval face outlined with shoulder-length dark hair cut to frame it perfectly. Thea had always made me feel like a hulking milkmaid to her dainty princess. I'd never known if the effect was intentional or a result of my own touchiness.

Now that I had the inside scoop on Thea's character, I could see how she achieved my displacement. She looked up, far more than she actually needed to, to make me feel even taller, and she pushed her cart with a little frown, as if it was almost too heavy to manage.

Thea's dark green dress was covered with teeny-weeny flowers in a sweet pink; nothing splashy or florid for Thea. She curled her lip at my workout clothes.

She guided her cart until she was at my side, right in the middle of the canned vegetables. I watched her lips curve in a venomous grin, and I knew she was about to say something she hoped would be painful.

So I beat her to the punch.

I leaned down to Thea and said with the widest smile I could stretch my lips into, "Drive past my house one more time and I'll have Claude Friedrich arrest you."

Thea's expression was priceless. But she snapped back together quickly.

"Marshall is mine," she hissed, reminding me vividly of my

seventh-grade school play. "You're trying to break up a happy marriage, you home-wrecker."

"Not good enough," I said. "You'd better warn Tom David to find another parking place."

Once again, Thea was disconcerted. But being Thea, belle of Shakespeare, she rallied.

"If you're the one leaving those awful things at my house"—and here she actually managed tiny tears—"please stop." She said this just loudly enough for an older lady who was comparing soup cans to absorb her meaning and then eye me in horror.

"What things?" I asked blankly. "You poor little gal, has someone been leaving things on your doorstep? What did the police say?"

Thea turned red. Of course she hadn't called the police; the police, in the person of Tom David Meiklejohn, had already been on hand.

"You know," I said, with as much concern as I could muster, "I'm sure Claude would station someone outside your house all night if you think there's a prowler." The older woman gave me an approving nod and ventured down the aisle to compare the prices of tomato sauce.

I hadn't said anything insincere in so long that it actually felt refreshing and creative.

Thea had to content herself with a low-voiced "I'll get you" and a flounce as she laboriously pushed her cart toward the meat counter. A very weak finale.

I left the grocery store with several bags, and I managed to feel almost like myself when I got home.

Damned if the chief of police wasn't still there. He'd just moved his car, probably to its parking space behind the apartments, but he'd returned his body to my carport. I pulled into my driveway and unlocked my trunk. I would not be kept out of my own home. Friedrich uncrossed his arms and sauntered over.

"What is it with you?" I asked. "Why do you keep turning up here? I didn't do anything."

"I might think I wasn't welcome if I didn't know better," Friedrich rumbled. "Your face is looking a lot better. How's the side?"

I unlocked my kitchen door and pitched in my purse and workout bag. I went back to the car for the first two bags of groceries. Friedrich wordlessly gathered the next two and followed me into the kitchen.

In silence, I put the cans away in the pantry, stowed the meat in the refrigerator, and slid the juice containers into the freezer of my side-by-side. When all that was done, when the bags were folded and put under the sink in their designated place, I sat down at my plain wooden table opposite Friedrich, who'd seated himself, and said, "What?"

"Tell me what you saw the night Pardon was killed."

I looked down at my hands. I thought it over carefully. My goal in keeping quiet had been to keep the police from asking questions about my past. Well, Friedrich had done that anyway, and been too trusting of his subordinates; my past was out, and the results hadn't been as dreadful as I'd always thought they would be. Or maybe I had changed.

If only Claude Friedrich was here to listen to me tell it, and I didn't have to go down to the police station again, why not tell him the little I knew?

And maybe Marshall had spooked me a little, with his "woman who knows too much" scenario.

Friedrich was waiting patiently. I would feel much more

comfortable in this big man's presence if I had nothing to conceal; he would then drench me with his warm approval. My mouth went up at one corner in a sardonic grin. This ambience was undoubtedly what made Claude Friedrich such a good policeman.

"I'll tell you what I saw, but it won't make any difference," I told him, making my decision abruptly. I looked him in the eyes and spread my hands flat on the table. "That's why I didn't see the need to tell you before."

"It was you that called me that night, wasn't it?"

"Yes. It was me. Partly because I didn't want him to lie out there all night, but mostly because I was scared some kids might find him."

"Why didn't you tell me all this to begin with?"

"Because I didn't want to come to your attention. What I saw wasn't important enough for me to risk you calling Memphis, getting the story about what happened to me. I didn't want people here to know. And yet it's happened, anyway." And I looked him directly in his eyes.

"That's a mistake I can't make up to you," he said. "I regret letting that report sit around on my desk, more than I can tell you. I'm taking steps to minimize the damage."

That was as much apology as I'd ever receive; and really, what more could he say?

I shrugged. My anger against him deflated gently. I had known all along that someday it was inevitable that my past would block my path again.

"What I saw was someone wearing a raincoat with a hood, wheeling Pardon over to the arboretum," I said flatly. "I don't know who it was, but I'm sure it was someone from the apartments. I figured you already knew that, since Pardon's body appeared and disappeared so many times. Gone when Tom O'Hagen paid his rent, back when Deedra paid hers. It had to have been hidden in a different apartment, though I can't imagine why anyone would move Pardon's corpse around."

"How was the body moved over to the arboretum?"

"It was in some garbage bags, one pulled on from the feet and another pulled on from the head. Then it was loaded in my garbage-can cart and rolled over there." I felt mad all over again when I thought of the use of my cart.

"Where are the garbage bags?"

"Gone to the incinerator."

"Why'd you do that?"

"My fingerprints were on them. I checked to see if Pardon was dead."

Friedrich gave me the strangest look.

"What?" I asked.

He shook his head. "Start at the beginning," he rumbled.

I began with my walk. Friedrich's eyebrows went up when he realized I walked by myself in the dead of night quite frequently, but he said nothing until I had given him the whole account.

"Do me a favor, Lily," he said finally.

I raised my eyebrows and waited.

"Next time, just call me to start with."

It took me a moment to realize he was joking. I smiled. He smiled back, no great big grin, but companionable. He was letting that warmth wash over me, and I was enjoying it just as much as any other suspect who'd just come clean. Why not? I thought, forgoing scolding myself for being a chump. I was prepared for Friedrich to take his leave, but there he stayed, seemingly content at my clean, bare kitchen table.

"So," the policeman said. "Happening in the same time frame, we have the murder of Pardon Albee and the strange persecution of Lily Bard and Thea Sedaka. Thea never called us in, officially. But Tom David said a few things to Dolph, who figured he better tell me. I like to know what's going on in my town. Don't you think it's strange, Lily, that so many unusual things are happening at the same time in Shakespeare?"

I nodded, though I had my own ideas about the "strange persecution." Moving quietly, I gathered my cutting board, a knife, and a package of chicken breasts. I began to skin and debone the chicken.

"The Yorks were gone on Monday. They returned that night late," Claude said. I worked and listened. "Mrs. Hofstettler was there all the time, but she's partially deaf and sometimes almost immobile. Jenny O'Hagen was at work, and Tom O'Hagen was sleeping. When he got up, he played a round of golf at the country club. He came home and went upstairs to pay blackmail to Norvel Whitbread, who was home from work 'sick.' Then Tom went down to pay his rent. You were unlocking the Yorks' apartment. When Tom found Pardon's door open, the body wasn't there, but the furniture was not in its usual order. An hour and a half later, Deedra came home from work, went upstairs to get her mother's check, then went down to pay the rent. And Pardon's traveling body was back on the couch, but arranged naturally enough that Deedra thought he was asleep."

"When did all the others pay their rent?" I asked over my shoulder as I scrubbed my hands at the sink. I thought this show-and-tell time was very strange, but I was enjoying it.

"I'd slipped my check under his door on my way to the station that morning," Friedrich said. "Norvel's rent was paid by the church. The secretary mailed Pardon a check, the Reverend McCorkindale told me. Marcus Jefferson says he'd also slid his rent check under Pardon's door on his way out to work that morning, and Pardon must already have made a trip to the bank right when it opened, because Marcus's check, mine, and Mrs. Hofstettler's were credited to Pardon's account when I called the bank."

"What about the one the church mailed?"

"Didn't get to Pardon's mailbox until the day after he died."

It would have been typical Pardon behavior to go by the church or up to Norvel's to ask about the rent, I thought, and raised my eyes to Friedrich's.

"But Norvel says Pardon didn't come to his apartment," the big man said, and I bent back to my work before I realized how strange the little exchange was.

"He's lying, though," I said.

"How do you figure?"

"Because Pardon did the vacuuming Monday himself. Remember the way the cord was wrapped? So he must have gone up to find out why Norvel hadn't done it. He's supposed to go in late to the church on Monday, after he's cleaned the apartment building's halls. The church gets a discount on his rent."

For the first time since I'd known him, Claude Friedrich looked surprised.

"How do you know all this, Lily?"

"If it's about cleaning, I know it. I think Pardon told me all that when he explained why Norvel was going to be cleaning the building instead of me." Pardon had just wanted to talk, as usual. It was fine with me not to have the poor-paying and tedious job of working under a constantly supervising Pardon.

Claude (as I now thought of him) looked at me a moment longer before resuming his running narrative of the day of the landlord's death. "So that morning Pardon stopped by Mrs. Hofstettler's to get her check, then went to the bank with three of the rent checks."

I put together a marinade and popped the strips of chicken breast in the bowl. I had a hankering for stir-fry tonight. I began to brown stew meat in a skillet while I chopped potatoes, carrots, and onions to go in the stew pot. I stirred the sauce for the tortilla casserole. I had some leftover taco meat to dump into the sauce, and a tomato, and after that I shredded three flour tortillas. I handed Claude the grater and the cheese. Obediently, he began to grate.

"How much?" he asked.

"Cup," I said, putting one on the table by him. "You were saying?"

"And he talked on the telephone several times," Claude continued. "He called the plant where Marcus works; we don't know who he talked to, there. Of course, that might be completely unrelated to Marcus. At least two hundred other people work there. About eleven, he called someone in rural Creek County, a pal he went to school with at UA, but the guy is on a business trip to Oklahoma City and we haven't been able to track him down yet."

I dumped all the stew ingredients into the slow cooker and got out my wok. While it was heating, I layered the tortilla casserole, including the grated cheese, and popped it in the freezer. Claude's voice provided a pleasant background sound, like listening to a familiar book on tape.

The stir-fry would provide two meals, I figured, the stew

at least three; one night, I would have a baked potato and vegetables; the remaining meal could be the tortilla casserole and a salad.

After I put the rice in the microwave, I began stir-frying the chicken and vegetables. I was hardly aware that Claude had stopped talking. I stirred quickly, conscious only of the quiet content that came when I was doing something I could do well. The rice and the meat and vegetables were done at almost the same time, and I faced a little dilemma.

After a moment's hesitation, since sharing this meal represented yet another disruption in my formerly pristine schedule, I got two plates out of the cabinet and heaped them with food, then put a fork, a napkin, and a glass of tea in front of the policeman. I set a plate in front of him, then put my own glass and fork on the table and retrieved my plate. I put the soy sauce within reach, added the salt and pepper, and sat down. I gave Claude a curt nod to indicate everything was ready, and he picked up his fork and began to eat.

I kept my eyes on my plate. When I looked up, Claude had finished his food and was patting his mouth with his napkin, carefully making sure his mustache was clean.

"Real good," he said.

I shrugged, then realized that was not a gracious response to a compliment. I forced my eyes to meet his. "Thank you," I said stiffly. Never had I felt my long abstinence from society more keenly. "Would you like some more?" I made myself add.

"No thank you, that was a gracious plenty," he responded correctly. "You finished?"

I nodded, puzzled. I found out why he'd asked in the next minute, when he reached across, took my plate and fork, and went to the sink. He turned on the faucets, located my dishwashing liquid, and began to wash all the dishes stacked on the counter.

I sat at the table with my mouth hanging open for a few seconds, then snapped out of my daze to get up and put away the leftovers in appropriate containers. Hesitantly, I set the now-empty wok by the sink for Friedrich to wash. I wiped the table and counters with a clean rag while he finished, and I swept the floor. Then, not knowing what else to do, I dried the dishes he'd put in the drainer and stowed them away.

The instant we were done with the homely procedure, before I could tense up again wondering what was to follow, Claude stuck out his huge hand, shook mine, and said, "I appreciate the good cooking. I get mightily tired of my own," and went to my front door.

I followed him as I ought to, but I wrapped my arms across my chest protectively. "Good-bye," I said, feeling I should say something more, but I couldn't think what. He gave me a totally unexpected smile, and I realized I'd never seen him like that, his wrinkles deepening as his lips curved up, his gray eyes suddenly slanting as the smile reached them.

"Good night, Lily," he rumbled, and then went down my driveway to the sidewalk. He turned toward the apartments. He didn't look back.

I shut the door, locked it mechanically, and went back to make sure the kitchen was spotless before going to bed. I was smiling, I saw in the bathroom mirror. I caught myself actually wondering what Claude Friedrich would be like in bed, and I shook my head at my reflection in the mirror. "You are going to the dogs, Lily," I said to the mirror. My face in the mirror looked rather pleased at the prospect.

Ten

The telephone rang while I was putting on my makeup. I blew out a breath of exasperation. I'd hoped with the new workweek beginning, my life would get back to normal.

"Yes?" I said curtly.

"Lily Bard?" asked a faintly familiar voice.

"Yes."

"This is Alvah York. T. L. and I just happened to remember yesterday that we owed you money."

"I can stop by this morning at ten-thirty." I'd be through with my first client by then.

"We'll be here."

As I checked my supplies and loaded my car, I wondered if I should ask the Yorks how their granddaughter was doing, or just ignore the subject. I'd feel more comfortable myself just ignoring it, I decided. It was time to get back to my old familiar distance.

As I was giving the Althaus home its weekly two hours (it could have used five, but the two was all the Althaus budget would stand), I thought long and hard about the people in the apartment building. One of those tenants had killed Pardon Albee, whose somewhat irritating presence was already growing faint in my memory. For all his petty faults—his enjoyment in knowing about the lives of other people, his determined gossip gathering—Pardon hadn't deserved what had happened to him.

While I scraped determinedly at a wad of chewing gum one of the many Althaus children had dropped on the kitchen linoleum, I pondered Pardon's violent death and the disrespect shown his body.

Once again, I wondered where that body had been hidden in its curious journeys.

Well, it could have been in the back of Pardon's own apartment. But surely Claude, who'd been so amazingly forthcoming the night before, would have told me if traces supporting that idea had been found. So the body had been close, but not in Pardon's own apartment. Not in the closet under the stairs; Pardon and I had apparently had the only keys, and the killer had not used Pardon's key, as the clean and orderly closet bore witness.

So, somewhere in the apartment house, or maybe in the garage? It seemed to me as if there was a thought in the back of my head, if I could just summon it up, something one of the tenants had told me, something that had made me wonder at the time . . . but God Almighty, I'd been talking to so many people lately. No wonder I couldn't remember. It would pop to the top of my mind if I just ignored it. I began thinking about hiding places for Pardon's body again.

I felt sure I could eliminate Mrs. Hofstettler's and Claude's apartments. Marie Hofstettler was very much on the ball despite her aches and pains—she'd have to be totally senile to miss a dead body—and Claude . . . just hadn't killed Pardon. I didn't know why I was so sure, but I was. The Yorks had been out of town until late. That left the O'Hagens—which meant Tom, since Jenny had been at work—Deedra Dean, Norvel Whitbread, and Marcus Jefferson.

As I plugged in the ancient Althaus vacuum cleaner, I thought about Tom O'Hagen. What if Tom had lied about Pardon's living room being empty? What if Pardon's body had been lying on the couch, as Deedra said it had an hour or so later?

I worked over that idea determinedly but got nowhere. I simply could not think of a good reason for Tom O'Hagen to lie about that. He could have said he thought Pardon was asleep, as Deedra had. He could have said everything looked as normal, so he assumed Pardon had stepped out or retreated to the bathroom for a moment. Instead, Tom had insisted the furniture had been moved, the throw rug rumpled, as if something had taken place in the room.

Finally, I abandoned Tom O'Hagen in disgust. It was Marcus Jefferson's turn in the lineup of suspects. Marcus was certainly strong enough to move Pardon's body. Marcus also had a grudge against Pardon; he obviously adored the little boy Pardon's policies prevented him from bringing home. But that was hardly sufficient motivation to strike Pardon hard enough to kill him, at least to my mind. I could only picture that happening if Pardon had provoked Marcus in some way—had threatened to tell Marcus's ex-wife that Marcus was having a fling with a white woman, say. Could Marcus's former wife have kept the child away from Marcus if she'd received that information? Would it make such a difference to her, in this day and age? And Pardon had called Marcus's workplace the day he died. But then, two hundred–odd people worked in the factory besides Marcus—among them, I recalled, was Deedra Dean's stepfather, Jerrell Knopp, whom I knew as an upright, polite, soft-spoken bigot, who would undoubtedly have violent feelings about any relationship his stepdaughter might have with a black man.

But Jerrell, if he killed anyone, wouldn't kill Pardon. He'd kill Marcus. Surely Marcus was supposed to work from eight to five? And Pardon had almost certainly died sometime before five. Marcus could have killed Pardon on his lunch hour, maybe. After all, if anyone had seen or heard from Pardon after the phone call he'd placed to his friend at eleven and Tom's knocking on Pardon's door at three, I hadn't heard about it.

Well, then, Deedra. Deedra had been at work until about 4:30. She'd left her job early to give Pardon her rent check. Every Shakespeare Garden Apartments tenant knew Pardon was a stickler for getting paid on the dot. Why would the living room be in disarray at three if Deedra killed Pardon later? I tried to picture Deedra enraged, Deedra lifting something heavy and striking her landlord the crushing blow that had killed him. What would Deedra lift? There was nothing at hand there by the door to the apartment, and I didn't think Pardon had been fool enough to stand talking to a young woman with a poker in her hand. Besides, if I knew Deedra, Deedra was more likely to vamp her way out of a bad situation than to resort to violence. I sighed. Scratch Deedra.

Then there was the hopeless, hapless Norvel, at this moment languishing—desolately, I hoped—in the Shakespeare jail, which was so outdated and decrepit that the town was wondering when, instead of if, it would be ordered to build a new one. Norvel was certainly dumb enough to commit murder at a time when other people were in and out of the apartment building. He was panicky enough to try to hide the body. He was prone to get angry enough to attack, as I knew from firsthand experience.

But though I tried to picture it while I gathered the wastebaskets from each room, I could not imagine anything Pardon could have on Norvel that would provoke Norvel to that much rage. Norvel was not especially strong after years of drinking, eating improperly, and avoiding hard work. The blow that had killed Pardon had been delivered by someone strong and someone furious. It could have been Norvel, by some extraordinary circumstance, but I was inclined to doubt it.

As I carried bags of garbage out to the Rubbermaid trash receptacles, dropped them in, and clamped the lids shut against loose dogs or raccoons, I felt glad I'd chosen housecleaning as my livelihood and not private detecting. This murder, I thought, pausing to stretch my back muscles, had been a murder of impulse, though whose impulse, I hadn't the foggiest notion.

Pardon had finally spoken the sentence, the one sentence in his lifetime of watching, prying, and telling, the hearer could not bear to hear.

And that person had struck two blows, the second one closing Pardon's mouth forever.

I locked the door to the Althaus home behind me, feeling satisfied at having, however temporarily, restored neatness to the Althaus's chaotic environment. I could not figure out the identity of the murderer of Pardon Albee, but I could bring order to chaos.

I actually work harder for Carol Althaus than for any client I have, because frankly, Carol arouses my pity, which is not an easy thing to do. Carol is a nice, plain woman coping with a blended family of two children of her own and two of her husband's, and Carol has limited brainpower to handle the load. She works hard at a low-paying job, comes home to try to feed and chauffeur four children under ten, and every now and then fields a phone call from her husband, whose job involves a lot of traveling. I often picture Jay Althaus in his quiet motel room, all alone, bed with clean sheets, TV with remote control that he alone wields, and contrast Jay Althaus's evenings with Carol's.

I had a break from 10:30 to noon; at noon, I'd clean a lawyer's office during his lunch hour. During this time every week, I usually run errands and pay bills. The first thing on my list for today was collecting the money owed me by the Yorks. As I drove back into town, for the very first time it occurred to me that Jay Althaus might be longing desperately for his wife and children every night he spends on the road.

Nah.

Rather than park on the street, which was too narrow for my comfort, I drove behind the apartment building. At this time of day on a weekday, there would be plenty of spaces empty.

Since I'd been considering the garage as a possible storage place for Pardon's body, I took the time to look it over. I pulled into Norvel's parking space—the apartment number is above each space, the effect remarkably like horse stalls at a big racetrack—and stood back to scan the white-painted wooden structure.

The garage, never a thing of beauty, didn't look its best empty. Since Shakespeare Garden Apartments doesn't have a basement, always a chancy thing in Arkansas, everyone in the building uses his or her stall for storage.

Starting from the left, the gap between the first stall and the fence surrounding the apartments was filled by the controversial York camper. The first stall is Norvel's. He doesn't own a car, but he'd leaned a broken framed mirror and a set of fireplace instruments in his allotted space: scroungings, I figured, that he hoped to sell. Marcus had put a wooden crate in the corner of his stall, and from it protruded a fat red plastic baseball bat and a tiny basketball goal. Claude Friedrich had put in a set of metal shelves that held car repair odds and ends and some tools. Deedra's space held a folded tent and a pair of muddy rubber boots. I have always thought it an odd sidelight to Deedra that she enjoys camping; of course, she doesn't enjoy camping alone. But it has always interested me that Deedra is willing to get away from her hot curlers for a weekend every now and then.

The first-floor tenants had scantier pickings. Marie has a car that I drive her around in, but other than that, her stall was empty. The Yorks, like Claude, have a set of shelves, but they were almost empty, and I thought they'd even been dusted; that was typical of Alvah. The O'Hagens had two expensive bicycles, covered with a tarp, at the back of their stall, and Pardon's car and a lawn mower were parked in his stall. I felt a little bleak as I looked at them. There is something melancholy about a dead person's possessions, no matter how impersonal they are, and there's nothing personal about a lawn mower.

This careful examination had told me absolutely nothing. The stalls are so open to view, it was hard to see how Pardon's body could have been hidden in any one of them. Maybe at the back of the stall between Mrs. Hofstettler's car and the wall? Or the same place in Pardon's stall? Those were the only two cars the killer could have counted on remaining in place. Self-consciously, I checked the two stalls. Not a stain or a thread from the green-and-orange shirt.

The camper would be a great hiding spot, but the Yorks had been driving it home at the time Pardon died.

Well, I had to get my money from those upright people. I turned to go into the building and got an unpleasant shock. Norvel Whitbread was standing in the doorway.

"How'd you get out?" I asked.

"Church put up my bail." He grinned at me, an unnerving sight, since Norvel is missing some teeth. Perhaps I'd knocked one of those out myself? I hoped so. His nose was many-colored and swollen.

"Get out of my way," I said.

"Don't have to. I live here and you don't." Norvel hadn't wasted any time consoling himself for his ordeal, I saw, and smelled.

"This time, the police won't come and I won't stop," I said.

I could tell from his eyes that Norvel had made up his mind to move, but before he could shift his feet, a shove from behind sent him flying out the door, staggering to keep his feet under him.

T. L. stood in the doorway, his arm still extended, his mouth in a tight line of anger.

"You piece of trash," he told Norvel, who had spun around to face this unexpected attack, "if the next landlord don't evict you, it won't be for lack of my trying. You leave this woman alone. I don't care where you go, but you get out of my sight."

T. L. was absolutely sincere, and that evidently impressed

Norvel, no matter what Norvel's condition was. He looked sullen, but he acted swiftly, heel-and-toeing it out of the parking area.

Now I had to thank T. L., and I didn't much want to.

"Lily, you probably wanted to get in a few more licks," T. L. said, with a smile that looked like his old self. "But I just can't sit still when I hear something like that. And I am the acting landlord. At least the lawyer asked me to lock the doors at night like Pardon did."

I had to smile. "I appreciate it, T. L.," I said.

"You come to see us? Alvah said you were going to drop by."

"Yep."

"Come on in."

The door to the York apartment was still open. I couldn't help glancing over at Pardon's. The crime-scene tape was still across the door. I followed T. L. into his living room, where Alvah was cross-stitching something blue and pink.

If T. L. was close to recovery, Alvah was not. I was sorry to see her face looked old, far older than it had the week before. She moved slowly and stiffly as she rose to get my money.

"Will you be needing me to help finish up?" I asked. I was babbling, but there was something awful and self-conscious about Alvah's sudden decline that made me want to fill the silence.

"I pretty much done it," Alvah said listlessly. But the curtains were still off the windows, and the ceiling fan above their little dining table hadn't been dusted, a quick look told me.

T. L. had sat himself down in his favorite chair, a leather easy chair with a pouch hanging over one arm that held a *TV Guide*, the remote control, and a *Sports Illustrated*. He opened the *Sports Illustrated,* but I had a feeling he wasn't really reading the page in front of him.

"Harley Don Murrell killed himself," Alvah said, handing me the money.

"Oh," I said slowly. "Well, that's . . ." My voice trailed off. I had no idea what that was. Good—a bad man dead? Bad—he hadn't had time to get the full horror of being in prison? A relief—their granddaughter no longer had to fear the day he got out on parole?

"How'd he do it?" I asked briskly, as if it mattered.

"He was on the third tier. He jumped over the rail and landed on his head." Alvah's eyes were fixed on my face, but I didn't think she was seeing me any more than T. L. was reading *Sports Illustrated.*

"Quick, then," I said, almost at random. "Well, see you soon."

I had barely cleared the door when I heard it close and lock behind me.

I was unnerved by this little exchange. I wondered what the Yorks' future would be like.

I went to the lawyer's office, and I cleaned, but I was absorbed in my thoughts the whole time and hardly remembered doing it afterward. I was recalled to my self when I nodded to his secretary on my way out the door. Now I had to drive two miles out of town to Mrs. Rossiter's. I had forgotten my earplugs, damn it.

Today was Durwood's biweekly bath. Durwood is Mrs. Rossiter's old cocker spaniel, and Mrs. Rossiter likes him to smell good, which is not a normal state for Durwood. When Mrs. Rossiter had fallen out with the local pet groomer, she'd been in a quandary, since Durwood doesn't travel by car well enough to handle a drive to Montrose. She'd been explaining her problem at her church-circle meeting, and God bless Mrs. Hofstettler, she'd chimed in to say she was sure Lily Bard could bathe that little dog.

Durwood isn't a bad dog, but bathing him is a hard job, and drying him is worse, to say nothing of cleaning the bathroom afterward. As I went to Mrs. Rossiter's front door, my rubber apron under my arm, I thought for the twentieth time that the worst thing of all was Mrs. Rossiter, who always regards Durwood's bath as a monologue opportunity, with me cast as the listener. I'd done everything in my not-inconsiderable power to quell the woman. It hadn't worked. And I didn't have my earplugs.

Mrs. Rossiter was off and running (at the mouth) the minute she came to the door. She told me I'd been beaten up by that drunk Norvel Whitbread, that the SCC people were saying it was because I'd made Norvel angry at church, though why that would make it okay for Norvel to hide in my yard and jump out at me, she couldn't figure.

When I'd filled Mrs. Rossiter's guest bathtub and set the shampoo handily within reach and pulled on my gloves, she told me that I lived next to Pardon Albee, who'd been murdered a week ago, and she'd heard I was seeing that strong young man who ran the health club, and did I know that he was still married to that cute little gal who worked at the SCC Day Care? Did I know that someone had left a rat on that gal's table, and written a dirty word in spray paint on her door?

I was only surprised Mrs. Rossiter didn't tell me I'd been raped in Memphis a few years ago.

By now I was soaping down the shivering Durwood. Letting Mrs. Rossiter's words run over me like water, I rubbed the lather gently through the dog's coat, wondering at the omission.

So far no one, *no one,* except for members of the Shakespeare Police Department, had mentioned Memphis to me or even looked at me as if they'd heard something. I simply couldn't believe that Tom David Meiklejohn, for instance, wouldn't want to share the sensational details with his drinking buddies—for that matter, wouldn't he enjoy even more giving the gory details to Thea?

I mulled this over while Mrs. Rossiter, perched on the closed toilet so she wouldn't miss a minute of my mute company, ran down the scale of gossip to arrive at her own blood pressure, which was always a prime topic.

I interrupted her once to ask her to turn on the ceiling heat lamp so Durwood could dry faster, and once again to ask her to pass me a towel that had fallen from its rack. By the time I'd gotten the dog dry and he'd pranced off with his owner to get a treat in the kitchen, I had arrived at the only possible reason the Shakespeare police force hadn't talked: Claude had threatened them with dismissal if they did. That was what he'd meant when he'd told me he was taking steps to minimize the damage he'd caused.

I shook gentle scouring powder into the fiberglass tub, having pulled the rubber mat off the bottom to pop into the wash pile on my way out. I scrubbed the tub slowly, turning this idea over in my mind. Though I rummaged through my brain, I could come up with no other solution that fit the facts.

After I'd cleaned up, Mrs. Rossiter handed me a twenty-dollar bill, and I nodded, my hand on the doorknob.

"See you in two weeks, won't we, Durwood?" she said,

looking down at the sweet-smelling Durwood. He looked as if he hoped not, but he wagged his tail, since she seemed to expect it.

The rest of the day was a slump time for me. I would see Marshall that night in class, and for the first time since I'd come to Shakespeare, I was not looking forward to it. I was grateful to Claude Friedrich for trying to make up for his error, but I didn't want to be. I couldn't be sure what his motive was. The stop at the Yorks' had upset me, not that I was bothered that a piece of trash like Harley Don Murrell was dead, but I hated seeing the Yorks in such a state.

There was nothing I could do about any of this.

I brooded my way through my last job, went home to get my gi, still dragging my feet. I even considered skipping class, a first. I couldn't quite bring myself to do that: It seemed like cowardice. But I deliberately waited till the last minute to go, so I wouldn't have to talk to Marshall before class began.

I had a definite feeling of deflation when I bowed and straightened and realized Marshall was not in the room. He'd been afraid to face me, too. Oddly enough, this made me feel good, proud.

"You leading class tonight?" I asked Raphael, the only student who has been there longer than I.

"That's what the man told me," he said, pleased under his offhandedness. "You gonna be okay? Your ribs? I heard you put that guy in the emergency room. Way to go, Lily!"

To my amazement, the other class members strolled up for their turn at congratulating me. I saw that from their point of view, my short skirmish with Norvel had validated what they were doing in the class, the time and pain they were expending to learn how to defend themselves. Janet Shook actually patted me on the shoulder. It was an effort to keep still. I took my place in line—first, tonight, since Raphael was facing us—in a daze. Whatever I had expected, this wasn't it.

Carlton was there again. Most people faltered after the second time, so I saw his attendance as a good sign. He wasn't quite as sore, I could tell by the way he moved, and he was stretching better. It wouldn't be long before he'd be able to do things that would amaze him. Raphael called us to attention, we bowed, and once again we began our uncomfortable routine.

Sit-ups reawakened the pain in my side, and I had to stop after thirty.

"Slacker," said Raphael, and Janet laughed. I told myself they were teasing, and made myself smile. Carlton came over and extended a hand to help me up, and, surprising even myself, I took it.

"Seriously, Lily, don't hurt yourself worse. Marshall told me to be sure and watch you don't overdo it," Raphael said as we drifted back in after our water break. I ducked my head to hide my expression and went back to my place, but when I faced forward for his next command, I saw Raphael looking at me with some speculation. We practiced some restraint moves, nothing I hadn't learned already. Everyone pretended to be scared to be my partner.

"So, woman of steel, when's your next match?" Carlton asked as we pulled on our shoes. He, Raphael, and Janet were the only ones left in the big room.

I actually laughed.

"You know, Norvel's already out on bail," I said, not knowing how to respond.

"Bet he won't be coming around you anymore," Janet said dryly. I figured she was still there because she was maneuvering to leave at the same time Carlton did, hoping for some significant exchange about meeting for a drink, maybe.

"Better not," I said sincerely. There was a little silence. They exchanged glances.

"Did you enjoy it, Lily?" Raphael asked suddenly. "I mean, here we practice all the time, spar all the time, have aches and pains that make my wife ask why I'm doing this. And me, big man, I've never been in a fight since I got out of junior high. But you, woman, you've done it. So how did it feel?"

"I'll tell you," I said after I'd thought for a moment. "It was scary and exciting and I could have hurt him real bad if the police hadn't shown up so quick."

"They pull you and Norvel apart?" Janet asked.

"No, I had him on the ground—bleeding. He was whipped. But I would have hurt him more." Raphael and Carlton exchanged uneasy looks. "It was the adrenaline," I tried to explain. "I had beaten a real man in a real fight, but he scared me, coming at me like that, unexpected. And since I was scared, I was mad. I was so mad at him for scaring me, I wanted to hurt him even worse." Admitting I'd been frightened wasn't too easy.

Raphael and Carlton were thinking over what I'd said, but Janet was after something else. "So it did work, all this training," she said, leaning forward to stare in my face. "You reacted just like you would in class, no freeze moment, the training kicked in." I could tell what she was scared of—not too hard to figure out.

And there was a short answer. "Yes, the training kicked in."

She nodded, a short, sharp bob of the head that signified confirmation of a deeply held hope. Then she smiled, a cold smile that made this shortish, ordinary woman something formidable. It was my turn to lean forward, and for once deliberately I looked someone else straight in the eyes, searching hers for what I suspected. I found it. I gave my own little nod. We were fellow survivors.

But we weren't going to talk about it. I wanted to avoid a girlish mutual emotional bath at all costs. It was something I couldn't bear. So I grabbed my stuff and mumbled something about going home to get cleaned up, said I was hungry.

I started thinking about Pardon's shirt on the way home. I've done laundry. I know the way clothes look when they've been washed hundreds of times. Pardon's shirt was a cheap shirt to begin with and he'd worn it and washed it repeatedly for years. It had been almost thin enough to read through. I remembered in my flashlight's beam seeing the ripped chest pocket. The threads had been frayed. I did not doubt that some of those threads remained at the site of Pardon's death, which had probably occurred in his apartment. More of them had to be at the place where his body had been stored. And where were his keys?

I prepared a baked potato and vegetables when I got home, but I hardly tasted the meal. That body had been hidden on the street I considered my turf. My cart had been used to haul Pardon to the dump site. Now that my mind was unclouded by thoughts of Marshall—or at least mostly unclouded—it began to run around the track of speculation about Pardon's death.

Suddenly, the parking garage popped into my mind. Something about it had sparked an uneasiness; something not as it was supposed to be? A memory jogged by something I'd seen there?

It bothered me while I washed my dishes, bothered me while I showered. I wasn't going to sleep. I put on black spandex shorts and a black sports bra, then pulled a red UA sweatshirt over that. Black socks and black cross-trainers completed my outfit. I punched in Claude's number, sure that if I heard his voice, I'd know what I wanted to tell him. But his answering machine came on. I don't leave messages on machines. I paced up and down my hall. I tried his number again.

Finally, I had to get out. Dark night. Cool air on my bare legs. Walking. It was a relief to be outside, to be silent, to be moving. I passed Thea's house without so much as a glance. And then I passed Marshall's. His car wasn't there. I walked on. I heard someone else coming on Indian Way and glided behind some azaleas. Joel McCorkindale ran by, wearing sweats, Nikes, and a determined expression. I waited till the sound of his running feet faded into the night before I stepped back out on the street.

The wind was blowing, making the new leaves rustle together, a sound almost like the sea.

I walked faster and faster, until I, too, was running down the middle of the street in silent Shakespeare, seeing no one, wondering if I were invisible.

I entered the arboretum from the far side, plunging into the trees and stopping to catch my breath in their concealment.

It came to me what I had to do. I had to go back to the garage. Looking at it would be better than visualizing. I would remember what had been niggling at me if I stood there long enough.

It was maybe 11:45 when I walked silently up the north side of the apartment driveway. I hugged the brick wall so anyone glancing out a window would not see me. I checked the lights. Mrs. Hofstettler's was out—no surprise there. A dim glow lit up the Yorks' bedroom window; maybe one of them was reading in bed. I had a hard time imagining that. Maybe a night-light? Norvel's second-floor apartment was dark, as was Marcus's.

As long as I was doing a bed check, I circled the building.

Of course Pardon's rooms were dark, and the O'Hagens'. Tom would still be at work and Jenny would have to be in bed at this hour. Upstairs, Deedra's lights were out. She was in bed either solo or duo. There was a light in Claude's bathroom window, so I walked around front to check his bedroom window. It was lit.

I didn't want to go in the building. I squatted and patted the ground around me until I found a rock the size of my thumbnail. I threw it at his window. It made quite a sound. I flattened myself against the wall again in case someone other than Claude had heard the noise. But no one came to see what it was, not even Claude.

All right, then, I'd remember on my own.

And suddenly, I did.

I'd have to go in the building after all. I moved around to the back door, taking a terrible chance. I pulled the key no one had thought to take away from me, the key to the back door, from my bra. I unlocked the door as quietly as it could be done, then went in. The stairs creak less by the wall, so I went up them quietly and carefully, one foot in front of the other. I passed Claude's door and went to Deedra's, decorated with a little grapevine wreath wrapped with purple ribbon and dried flowers. I knocked quietly.

The door opened so quickly, I was sure Deedra had been lying on the floor right inside it, with company. In the light falling through from the hall, I could see a male leg, and since it was dark, I deduced that Marcus Jefferson had succumbed to temptation once again.

Deedra looked very pissed off, and I couldn't blame her, but I didn't have time for it.

"Tell me again what you told me—about when you came home from work early to give Pardon the rent check."

"I swear to God you are the weirdest cleaning woman in Arkansas," Deedra said.

"Talk to me. For once, I want to listen."

"Will you go away right after? No more questions?"

"Probably."

"Okay. I came home from work. I ran upstairs to get the check Mama had given me. I took it down to Pardon's. The door was a little open. He was lying on the couch, his back to the door. The area rug was all rumpled and the couch was crooked. I said his name, I said it a lot, but he didn't move. I figured he'd maybe had a drink and passed out or he was taking a hell of a nap, so I just put the check on his desk, to the left of the door. This what you want?"

I beckoned to her to keep on.

"So . . . so then, I . . . well, I went back and got in my car. I had to go back to work even though I just had a few minutes left. You wouldn't believe how ticky Celie Schiller is. . . ."

"Lower your voice and speed up," I suggested quietly.

"My maid tells me what to do," she told the air, "Incredible."

But she looked in my face and went on. "And then I got in my car . . . and I backed out of my place, and put it in drive to go out, and I had to go out careful because of the Yorks' stupid camper. . . ."

I held a finger to my lips. Her voice was rising.

"That's what I wanted," I whispered.

"Oh, don't want to hear about the run in my hose that day?" she asked with killing sarcasm, then shut the door firmly in my face.

I ran my fingers through my hair and gripped two handfuls of it. I stood there thinking, my eyes closed, still facing Deedra's door. I took a few steps down the hall and tapped Claude's door with one finger. I couldn't risk more.

No answer. I turned the handle. Locked, of course.

I went back down the stairs quietly. Even if I'd been standing in the bottom hall, I wouldn't have heard me.

I didn't know why I was so tense, why my mission seemed so urgent. But I never ignore the back of my neck, and the skin of it was crawling. There was tension in the air. In the silent building, the air was humming with it. I opened the door with a feeling of relief to be getting out, and I eased through the opening as silently as I could manage. I re-locked the door behind me.

Going from the lighted hall to the relative gloom of the parking area cost me some vision, and I stood still to let my eyes adjust. Pardon had installed one all-night security light in the middle of the garage, and it lit up that immediate area like stage lighting. But the illumination didn't extend to the end stalls. I skirted the edge of the light and drifted to the outside wall of the garage. For maybe five minutes, I stood in the darkness, listening. I shifted my foot, and something clinked.

Slowly, I crouched down in the weeds that had found life against the wall of the garage, sprouting through cracks in the pavement. I patted the ground gently. My fingers found a familiar shape, traced it. I tried to pick up what I'd found all in one piece, so it wouldn't jingle. I held it up close to my face. Pardon Albee's key ring. I had nowhere to put it; there were at least fifteen keys on the metal circle. The safest place was where they'd been, so I gently laid them back in the weeds, where they'd been since the day he died.

Nothing moved. I didn't hear anything but the faint sound of a car cruising by in the street. Even that died away. But as quiet as it was, I knew there were people near. I could feel the hair standing up on the nape of my neck. So I slowly rose to my feet, nearly moved away to the safety of my house, wondered if I would make it.

I extended my hand to the knob on the camper. It was in the camper that Pardon's body had been concealed; if any evidence remained, it would be in that little space.

The Yorks hadn't been due home until night. But they'd come home earlier, the day Pardon had died. I knew it.

And then I turned the knob. The door popped open with a click, and just as I took in a breath of triumph, a huge shape launched itself at me from the black interior.

I didn't have a chance to defend myself. In ferocious silence, I was being beaten, and I needed all my breath to fend off the blows, to keep the fists from killing me. I knew only one person was there, but it was a person possessed of a demon, a man who seemed to have more than two hands.

I had to fight back or I would die, but the frequency and

pain of the blows left me scant brainpower. I formed a fist and struck the first thing I could see, some ribs, not an effective blow, but a start, a gesture. I was weakening and soon I would be down on the ground, and it would be all over if I fell. It was almost a miracle I'd managed to keep on my feet as long as this.

Then I caught a glimpse of exposed neck and drove the edge of my hand in as hard as I could. My attacker gave a grunt and faltered, and I thrust-kicked with all my strength, not really caring where it landed as long as it sank into him. He staggered, and I could take a deep breath, and then a voice behind me said, "Stop right there."

Who? Who should stop? My attacker was in no doubt, and he threw himself at the source of the command, again moving so quickly and with so much determination that the speaker and I were unprepared.

The struggle came into the light, moving toward the center of the parking area, and I could see T. L. York and Claude rolling on the ground, struggling for a gun that I thought must be in Claude's hand. Their hands and legs were so confused and I was so dazed by the suddenness of all this that for a second I stood staring blankly, as if I had no stake in the outcome. I was weak enough to be shaking, but I had to move, to help—whom?

"Lily!" Claude said, in what he maybe intended as a shout, and that decided me. Only the innocent one would want my help.

I circled them, looking for my chance. It came when T. L. rolled on top of Claude, still gripping both Claude's wrists. I leaped in to straddle them, grabbed T. L. by his hair with one hand and cupped his chin with the other, and pulled back hard, almost hearing the faint echo of Marshall's voice adjuring me to be careful practicing this in class, since a wrong move could cause serious injury.

Well, this was serious-injury time. I twisted his head and pulled up. You have to follow your head. The rest of his body had to come up, too, or his neck would break. With a howl, he let go of Claude and raked backward, trying to get me off him, but I had my fingers sunk in his still-thick hair. In agony, he reared back, but my legs were locked on either side of him, I was gripping him with my knees, and the only way he could get rid of me was to do what he did next—fall backward on top of me. I wrapped my legs around him as he left the ground and heaved back, and I never loosened my grip on his head. I began squeezing with my strong legs, my ankles crossed over his gut, and he rolled from side to side trying to dislodge me.

"Hold still, goddamn it!" said a voice I could hardly recognize as Claude's, and again I didn't know if he meant me or T. L. I didn't have a lot of options, since I couldn't breathe and I could tell only my own rage was keeping me attached to him.

Then the gun went off. It was deafening. T. L. screamed, and since my grip had loosened at the shock of the sound, he could roll off me and continue to scream. Suddenly, I could breathe. I didn't feel like getting up, though. It was enough to lie on the filthy concrete and look up at the moths circling in the light.

Eleven

I wasn't in the hospital, but I was under house arrest.

The chief of police had confined me to my own home for a week. He had coaxed Mrs. Hofstettler into calling all my clients and explaining (as if they hadn't heard) that I'd been a little hurt and had to recuperate. I told Mrs. Hofstettler, via Claude, to tell them I didn't expect to get paid, since I wasn't going to work. I don't know if she passed the message along. Everyone sent me a check but the Winthrops, which figured. However, Bobo came by to bring me a fruit basket he said was from his mother. I was sure he'd bought it himself.

Marshall really had gone out of town; he wasn't just avoiding me. He called me from Memphis to tell me his father had had a heart attack and he and the rest of his family were just circling the hospital room in a holding pattern, waiting to see what would happen. I assured him several times that I would be all right, and after I'd detailed my wounds to him and explained what I was doing for their treatment, he seemed satisfied I would live. He called me every other day. I was stunned to receive flowers with his name on the card. He was eloquently silent when I told him Claude was with me one night when he called.

Mrs. Rossiter brought the damn dog by to see me. Claude told her I was asleep.

Carrie Thrush paid me a house call.

"You should be in the hospital," she said sternly.

"No," I said. "My insurance won't cover enough of it."

She didn't say any more after that, since she wouldn't question me about my finances, but all the medicine she gave me was in sample boxes.

Claude came every day. He had gone with me in the ambulance to the hospital, following the one carrying T. L.

He had shot T. L. in the leg.

"I wanted to hit him in the head with the pistol butt," he said when we were waiting for the doctor in a white cubicle that night. I was glad to listen to him talking, so I wouldn't moan and disgrace myself. "I've never shot anyone before— at least to actually hit them."

"Um-hum," I said, concentrating fiercely on his voice.

"But I was sure I would hit you instead, and I didn't want to beat up my ally."

"Good."

"So I had to shoot him." His big hand came up to touch my shoulder, stroke it. That hurt like hell. But I didn't say anything.

"Why were you there?" I asked after a long pause.

"I'd been staking out the camper for the last week."

"Oh, for God's sake," I said, thinking that all my inspiration had been for nothing, Claude had been there mentally before me.

"No, I thought that someone else had killed Pardon, not

T. L. I thought the Yorks didn't want to tell anybody Pardon's body had been in their camper, but I didn't think they had put him there."

"The curtains," I said.

"Curtains? What curtains?"

But by then the doctor had come in and told Claude he had to step outside. It was the emergency room doctor, who'd just finished sending T. L. up to the operating room. His eyebrows flew up when he saw my scars, but for once I didn't care.

"Your X rays," he said.

"Mmm?"

"You have no broken bones," he said, as if that was the most amazing thing he'd ever heard. "But many of your muscles are badly strained. You are very thoroughly bruised. But I can tell you're a workout buff; underneath all that, you're physically fit. Normally, I'd put you in the hospital, just for a night or two, just as a precaution. What do you think?" He observed me closely from behind glasses that reflected the glaring overhead light. His ponytail was caught up neatly in an elastic band at the nape of his neck.

"Home," I said.

"Anyone there to take care of you?"

"I am," rumbled Claude from outside the curtain.

I opened my mouth to protest, but the doctor said, "Well, if you have someone to help . . . Believe me, you're not going to be able to get to the bathroom without help for a few days."

I stared at him, dismayed.

"You have some healing injuries. You seem to be prone to get into trouble," the doctor observed, sticking his pen behind his ear.

I heard Claude snort.

I had a couple of emergency room pain pills, and Carrie came by and supplemented. Claude proved to be an unexpectedly good nurse. His big hands were gentle. He knew about the scars beforehand from the Memphis police report, which was good, because there was no way I could conceal them from someone who helped me with a sponge bath. He also helped me hobble to the toilet, and he changed my sheets. The food I'd frozen ahead came in very handy, since I couldn't stand long enough to cook, and when I was by myself, I could take my time getting to the kitchen to heat it up.

A couple of times, Claude brought carryout and we ate together, the first time in my bedroom—he improvised a bed tray—and the second time, I was able to sit at the table, though it exhausted me.

The swelling was almost gone and I had evolved from black and blue to sickly shades of green and yellow when we finally talked about the Yorks.

"How did you come to be watching?" I asked him. I felt good. I'd just taken a pain pill, I was clean and my sheets were clean, and I'd managed to brush my hair. I lay there neatly, my hands resting by my sides, a little sleepy and relaxed. That was as good as it got, that week.

"I went over everyone's statement several times. I drew up a timetable, and a list of alibis; it was just like a TV special," he said, his legs extended comfortably in front of him, his fingers laced across his belly. He'd hauled the armchair into my bedroom.

"Marcus was my hottest suspect for a long time," he continued. "But he just couldn't have left work—too many witnesses. Deedra, too. She was gone from work for maybe thirty minutes, and she was out on a date while Pardon's body was being dumped. After you told me exactly when that was," and he shot me a mildly reproachful look, "I could eliminate her. Marie Hofstettler is just too old and infirm. Norvel was a possibility, and Tom O'Hagen. But Tom was at work when Pardon was killed, and Jenny was working at the country club on decorations for the spring dance . . . lots of witnesses. She couldn't have killed Pardon.

"And I didn't think it was you, at least not after a few days."

"Why?" The pill was taking effect, and I was only mildly interested in the answer.

"Maybe because the only secret you'd kill for is what happened to you in Memphis. And when I let it slip, you didn't try to kill me."

I was faintly amused. I looked off in a corner.

"So that left Norvel," I said quietly.

"Unless the Yorks had come home early."

"I would have picked Norvel."

"I couldn't decide. In a way, it seemed too smart for Norvel to think of. But in a way, it seemed exactly like Norvel, drunk. Wavering between one hidey-hole and the next. Moving Pardon here. Moving him there. We looked in every apartment in the building, in one way or another."

I wasn't going to ask questions.

"No traces of the body anywhere. He'd bled a little from the mouth. No hairs, and the only fibers on the body were from a cotton blend, deep red and bright gold and blue."

"Alvah's curtains," I murmured.

"I didn't know about Alvah's curtains," Claude rumbled.

"But I didn't see anything in anyone else's apartment that came close to matching those."

I remembered him walking through my house the first time he'd come in. He'd been looking for something that would ring a bell.

"We went all over the parking stalls, trying to find one that could have been used for the body. No luck there. I saw you looking that day, and I wondered what you were up to."

"Saw me from where?"

"Pardon's apartment. I'd been sitting in it some days and every night, watching people go in and out and do their curious things, and trying to get some idea of where to take this."

I was definitely feeling dimmer.

"We'd searched the garbage the day Pardon's body was found."

I smiled to myself.

"We'd looked in every apartment. We'd kept a watch on the movements of everyone for a day or two, then only on Norvel and the Yorks."

"Not a close enough watch on Norvel."

"Goddamn it, Lily, he goes out walking, we don't know he's got a ski mask stuffed in his pocket. He must have stuck the broom handle by the fence earlier in the day. I never saw him with it."

"But that was how you were able to get there so fast. You were awake. Did you pull your shirt off on purpose?"

"Yeah," he confessed, looking embarrassed. "I thought it would look more like I'd been wakened by you yelling."

"So, you were watching the Yorks and Norvel."

"I'd caught Deedra's reference to the camper, too. She might have gotten confused. She pulls in and out of the parking lot every day. But she sounded sure. I couldn't grill her without even her getting the drift, but the more I thought about it, the more possible I thought the Yorks' presence was. I called the Creek County courthouse. Harley Don Murrell's trial was over in time for the Yorks to have driven home. I checked with their daughter over there, real casually, and she said they'd left at one, right after lunch, too upset to stay any longer. Alvah and T. L. had said they'd stopped at the Hillside flea market and walked around a little to stretch their legs, but if that wasn't true, they could have gotten here before three."

"They did. Alvah had watered the plant in the kitchen. It was wet when I went to water it at three," I said. "Her bedroom blinds were open. Those were the things she did when she first came home. And her living room curtains were down. I didn't notice that day, but I did notice on Wednesday. I thought Alvah had started spring cleaning, but T. L. wrapped the body in them." That, I had figured out all by myself.

Claude stretched his long arms above his head and lapsed back into his former position. "Alvah told me today that when they got back to Shakespeare, she went in the apartment with her suitcase and left T. L. unloading the rest of the stuff. She watered the plant and opened the blinds." He tipped an imaginary hat to me.

"Outside, she could hear voices. Their door was open, and so was Pardon's; T. L. had stopped by to pay the rent. Pardon had found out about the trial and the verdict from his friend in Creek County, but instead of consoling the Yorks over the difficulty of living through a trial like that, Pardon chose to quote what Murrell's wife had said about the Yorks' granddaughter. And after the worst day of his life, T. L. just couldn't take it. T. L. and Pardon exchanged words, and he hit Pardon in the mouth. Pardon jumped back and bumped into the couch. It was like running from a hostile dog. T. L. went after him. He was going to hit Pardon in the jaw, but Pardon turned and slipped, and he hit Pardon in the neck with his fist, as hard as he could. It crushed Pardon's throat."

"And they put him in the camper," I said.

"Yep. T. L. ran into his apartment, past Alvah, ripped down the curtains without asking her, and ran back in to Pardon's place. Alvah followed. They loaded Pardon into the camper, wrapped in the curtains—his keys fell out then—and they drove around with him for a little while. They were completely panicked. They couldn't decide what to do. The Yorks had never broken the law in their lives. They were going to dump him by a back road, to make it seem he hadn't been killed by an apartment resident. But they realized they could establish an alibi, since no one had seen them return, if Pardon's body was found closer to the apartments to make that alibi valid.

"While they were driving around with Pardon's body, Tom went to Pardon's apartment to pay his rent. Door unlocked, no Pardon. Then the Yorks returned, pulled right up to the back door, opened the camper door, stowed Pardon back in his apartment."

"How come they didn't hear Deedra knock on his door?" I asked.

"Alvah got nauseated," Claude said, looking down at his hands. "She had to run in her place to the toilet and T. L. went with her. While Alvah was being sick, Deedra left for work. They never knew she'd seen the camper—lucky for Deedra. When Alvah was better, they drove away again. They didn't think about disposing of the curtains he'd been wrapped in. They didn't think about the threads from his torn pocket getting left in the camper. They didn't think about people trying to pay their rent, not finding Pardon in his place. And they couldn't lock the door to Pardon's apartment because they had to get back in, and they couldn't find Pardon's keys."

"They evidently drove around in a daze, and just came home when they'd originally intended to, between seven and eight at night. They put the rest of their gear into their place. They'd been talking, of course, and they'd decided Pardon had to be found somewhere close to his apartment, some place he could've walked, but also some place he could have chanced across a mugger. The arboretum was the logical place, maybe the only sane choice the Yorks made. T. L. remembered your garbage-can cart. He'd seen it sitting by the curb on garbage days and always kind of coveted it. . . . So he waited, thinking no one in Shakespeare would be up that late. And he was nearly right."

"When did you decide it wasn't Norvel?"

"When I saw T. L. come out of the camper at you." He smiled at me, making fun of himself. "I'd thought maybe Norvel had just used the camper to stow Pardon's body and that the Yorks were so afraid of looking guilty that they were covering that up. I didn't want it to be the Yorks."

"I knew it was the Yorks," I said calmly. "Because of the curtains."

"You figured it out that way?"

"If Alvah's curtains were missing, there had to be a reason. And only T. L. would grab curtains down from their hooks. If Alvah had known what he was doing, she would have run gotten a sheet or tablecloth that I wouldn't've missed. But I missed the curtains," I said drowsily, "and I knew someone had watered the plant."

"Why . . . Lily, why did you go to the camper?"

"I wanted to see what was in it," I said, and let my eyes close.

"Oh, yeah," I said thickly, hauling my lids up again. "How come you didn't know T. L. was in there?"

"I did," he said, trying not to sound angry with me. "I was waiting for him to come out with some evidence. He couldn't destroy it in the camper; he would've had to take it into the apartment. I couldn't get a warrant to search the camper. I didn't have enough evidence."

"'Kay. My mind's at rest."

"One more thing."

"Mmm?"

"What about the handcuffs on the Drinkwaters' steps, Lily? What about the dead rat?"

"Oh, that was Thea. I was pretty sure as soon as Marshall told me what her secret life was like. And I knew for sure after I realized you'd threatened everyone who worked for you with death if they talked about what happened to me. But Tom David had already told his honey bunch. He didn't let her tell anyone else. But she knew, and she wanted to torment me. Once I figured that out, I didn't worry about it anymore. I can handle ole Thea."

I rolled an eye at Claude.

"Secret life?" he said hopefully. "Thea Sedaka has a secret life?"

"Maybe tell you sometime," I said.

"I hear Marshall's coming back tomorrow, Lily," Claude said when I was almost drifting off. "What are you going to do?"

"Go to sleep," I mumbled, and did.